St. Maryan Seven The Westgate Rescue

St. Maryan Seven Series, Volume 2

Jorges P. Lopez

Published by Jorges P. Lopez, 2023.

This is a work of fiction. Similarities to real people, places, or events are entirely coincidental.

ST. MARYAN SEVEN THE WESTGATE RESCUE

First edition. November 18, 2023.

ISBN: 979-8224120994

Written by Jorges P. Lopez.

Also by Jorges P. Lopez

A Guide Book to H R ole Kulet's Blossoms of the Savannah
H R ole Kulet's Blossoms of the Savannah: Plot Analysis and Characters
H R ole Kulet's Blossoms of the Savannah: Themes and Elements of Style
H R ole Kulet's Blossoms of the Savannah: Answering Excerpt & Essay Questions
H R ole Kulet's Blossoms of the Savannah: A Complete Guide

A Guide Book to Margaret A Ogola's The River and the Source
The River and the Source: Plot Analysis and Characters
The River and the Source: Themes and Elements of Style
Margaret Ogola The River and the Source: Answering Excerpt & Essay Questions
Margaret Ogola The River and the Source: A Complete Guide

A Guide to Adipo Sidang's Parliament of Owls
Adipo Sidang Parliament of Owls: Plot Analysis and Characters
Adipo Sidang's Parliament of Owls: Themes and Elements of Style

Adipo Sidang's Parliament of Owls: Answering Excerpt and Essay Questions

A Guide to Bertolt Brecht's The Caucasian Chalk Circle
The Caucasian Chalk Circle: Plot Analysis and Characters
The Caucasian Chalk Circle: Themes and Elements of Style
Bertolt Brecht's The Caucasian Chalk Circle: Dealing with Excerpts & Essay Questions
Bertolt Brecht The Caucasian Chalk Circle: A Complete Guide

A Guide to Henrik Ibsen's A Doll's House
Henrik Ibsen's A Doll's House: Plot Analysis and Characters
Henrik Ibseb's A Doll's House: Themes and Elements of Style
Henrik Ibsen's A Dolls House: Answering Excerpt & Essay Questions

A Guide to Kazuo Ishiguro's An Artist of the Floating World
An Artist of the Floating World: Plot Analysis and Characters
An Artist of the Floating World: Themes and Elements of Style
Kazuo Ishiguro's An Artist of the Floating World: Answering Excerpt & Essay Questions

A Guide to Reading A Silent Song and Other Stories ed. by Godwin Siundu
A Silent Song and Other Stories Edited by Godwin Siundu : Volume One

A Silent Song and Other Stories edited by Godwin Siundu : Volume Two
A Silent Song and Other Stories edited by Godwin Siundu : Volume Three

A Guide to Reading John Lara's The Samaritan
Reading John Lara's The Samaritan: Plot Analysis and Characters
John Lara's The Samaritan: Themes and Elements of Style
John Lara's The Samaritan: Answering Excerpt and Essay Questions

A Study Guide to Paul B. Vitta's Fathers of Nations
Paul B. Vitta's Fathers of Nations: Plot Analysis and Characters
Paul B. Vitta's Fathers of Nations: Themes and Elements of Style
Paul B Vitta's Fathers of Nations: Answering excerpt & Essay Questions

Essay Writing
The A to Z Basic Composition Writing Skills
Writing the Grade A Essay

JIMMY DIARIES SERIES
Jimmy Karda
Jimmy and his Ancestor
Jimmy and the Ramshackle
Jimmy and the Covid 19 Scare
Jimmy and the Dodger

Jimmy and the Tasty Buns

Poetry
Silent Musings : Poetry
Silent Musings: Poetry

Reading John Steinbeck's The Pearl
John Steinbeck's The Pearl: Plot Analysis and Characters
John Steinbeck's The Pearl: Themes and Elements of Style
John Steinbeck's The Pearl: Answering Excerpt and Essay Questions
John Steinbeck's The Pearl: A Complete Guide

Short Stories
Beauty's in a Mark
To Be a Groom

St. Maryan Seven Series
Amy
St. Maryan Seven The Westgate Rescue
St. Maryan Seven and the Dubai Allure
St. Maryan Seven and the Soccer Affair

Understanding Poetry
The Elements of Poetry: A Comprehensive Course for High Schools and Colleges

Notes on Jorges P Lopez's The Elements of Poetry

ST. MARYAN SEVEN
And The
WESTGATE RESCUE

FIRST EDITION

1st Printing 2019
ISBN:

MIDAS TOUCH PUBLICATIONS
P.O.BOX 253-00610
NAIROBI.
Tel: 0733 952 552
E-MAIL: midas14@gmail.com
First Printed in Kenya

ST. MARYAN SEVEN
And The
WESTGATE RESCUE
Jorges P. Lopez

Let us console all those

Who fell at Westgate; this one's
A song of mourning to their loved ones;
Oh Lord we ask you give them peace that grows
From your eternal kindness; save their sons
And daughters endless throes.

For Polly

Prologue

The girl walked down the passage between the left and the middle rows of desks to the teacher's table. She paused there and looked comically at some part of the back of the class, then moved over to the front of the right column to stand in front of another dark girl.

'Hi Stella,' she said looking at the other girl like she was the class teacher about to give a lecture. 'I'm here to pick up my book,' she said. She adjusted imaginary glasses, bent her head low and looked 'over' the glasses at the other girl, then she took a large volume of *Prentice Hall Literature* that lay on the other girl's desk and lifted it up in the air. She lifted her face to look at the volume raised high up in the air, then put it back on the desk again. The other girls looked on mesmerized.

'Thanks Stella,' she said putting the book back on the desk again. 'I'll be here this afternoon to pick it up again.' She smiled at the other girl. The rest of the class cracked up, then suddenly went quiet. The laughter was too short lived. The girl at the front readjusted the imaginary glasses and looked at the class above them.

'What!' she said, making sure they understood it was not a question. It was then that she realized they were not looking at her; they were looking at the door. She darted her eyes there quickly and saw Mr. Maranga, their History teacher, standing there. He was leaning on the door frame looking at her in an amused manner, his hands folded across his chest.

'Nice antiques Miss Manji,' he said delightedly. 'I'm not sure I shouldn't tell on you to your class teacher; shouldn't she know what you are up to over here?'

The girl called Manji froze for a split second like a mouse caught in a drawer as sweat broke out of her hairline, then she dashed back to her desk and the class burst into renewed laughter.

Mr. Maranga gave his class time to adjust before he introduced, then plunged into the new lesson.

'So what role has fundamentalism played in the history of religions?' he asked as he faced the class. It might have been the resurgence of violence in the Middle East that sparked the idea in him or the general state of the country with calls by Al-Shabaab to punish the country for invading Somalia. Nobody could tell for sure. But Mr. Maranga taught History that way; he always looked for an interesting mundane issue related to the topic at hand and began with it. By the time the topic began per se, all his students would be all ears. 2W was a favourite class of his for despite the apathy that many girls tended to have towards History at St. Mary's – the arts tend to be the bane of many students who consider themselves scientists - 2W remained lively and therefore made his lessons worth his while. It was also probably the mutuality between his way of teaching and the nature of 2W; the girls liked the way he taught and therefore they were both attentive and participated more than they would have done with another teacher. As usual, he sat on the teacher's table facing the class. The sleeves of his sky blue shirt which had been severely ironed were rolled back to the elbows revealing the bulging muscles of the lower arms. His arms were crossed across his chest, his head hanging so that his chin which desperately begged for a shave fell on his chest. None of the girls looked eager to answer his question so he fell on his last resort; he picked on a student to initiate conversation. Naturally, his eye fell on Miss Manji.

'Miss Manji,' he said looking at the short Indian girl who was a little plump. Her round cheeks had a slight touch of pink pimples and so did her forehead. Her friends simply called her Raj. 'Yes Miss Manji, what religion do you subscribe to?'

The girl looked up quickly like a three-year-old caught with her hand in the sugar jar. She did not smile as she said, 'I'm Muslim.'

'Muslim? Not Hindu? Interesting. Do you know when Islam came about?' he asked her hastening as though no grass would be let to grow under the feet now that the topic was underway.

'I'm not very sure,' the girl said.

'Let's try another angle,' Mr. Maranga said looking at the girl not unkindly. 'Islam has been accused of fomenting fundamentalism. Do you think it is fundamentalist?'

'Depends on what you call fundamentalism,' the girl said as she narrowed her eyes, her mind fully brought back to class. 'I believe that Islam is the only true religion and although I don't support forceful conversion into Islam, I think all human beings should be taught the true religion. Islam is not in the same league with other religions.'

'Who knows which one is the true religion?' a big dark girl to the right of the class asked.

Her name was Valerie Chimaka but she was simply 'Mak' to all the other students in 2W. She had her roots somewhere in Nigerian. Her parents lived in Nairobi where they had a jewelers business somewhere in Westlands, a suburb in the western outskirts of the capital city. In class, she was often careful to avoid the 'o' with which she punctuated her normal chit-chat. She was a darling of her class because she was the usual joker when the teachers were not around. Behind her back, her backtrackers said that her pet-name fit her for she was as big as a Mack truck.

'Indeed who does?' the teacher echoed her.

'The Koran teaches that Islam is and being Muslim, that is all I need to know,' Raj said.

'Fundamentalism is wrong,' another girl to the left said. 'People should be left free to decide what and how to worship without being intimidated. Besides, everybody talks about changing the world but nobody talks of changing herself.'

'Yeah, and those people include Muslims themselves. They should also be left free to live in their own land in peace without fear of being forcefully evicted or killed like it happens in the West Bank and the Gaza,' Raj said; there was no anger in the voice this time, just a simple statement of fact. A number of girls looked at her as if she was not in her right mind.

Although she wasn't a great talker, it was common knowledge that Raj defended her religion fiercely, probably because religion at St. Mary's largely meant being a Catholic or a saved Christian. Those who were neither of these were forced to follow the Christian routine on Sunday morning when Christians congregated at the Shah Hall. They were often pissed off for they were obligated to gather in some room or other and pretend to do something though it was as clear as daylight that they would have preferred to pick their own days and modes of worship. Some girls would have considered Raj fundamentalist if they had looked at the term from Mr. Maranga's point of view, that is, from his definition of it. All the same, Raj was one of the darlings of 2W, and indeed the whole school. She was all things to all people and had an engaging manner with students which made even the meanest girls think twice before they treated her ill. She made friends as easily as she kept them. She was also bright. She was a dab hand at the sciences and was able to remain among the top girls in Form Two without appearing to try. All other girls in Form Two had given up the top position in both Physics and Maths to her. Part of her friendship with other girls sprang from the fact that she was very ready to help other girls who had a problem in these subjects and as a result, both teachers and students found her indispensable. She and Amy had so recently made Jenny – a girl who had always been an 'also ran' - a household name when her marks shot from thirty-one to eighty nine, winning her the Best Improved Junior Science Student Medal. Jenny's name was still on everyone's lips. Raj's only Achilles' heel appeared to be her soft spot in defending her religion which she did as if she was worried that if she didn't, she was in real danger of being converted to something else. Like they say, you can't win them all. Not that it happened often, this kind of defense mechanism that is, for apart from her tendency to play pranks in class, a job clearly up her alley, she was otherwise a quiet girl. You could however see that her arguments weren't a patch on the other girls'.

'All religions have been fundamentalist at one time or other,' Mr. Maranga was saying. As usual, he went the extra mile to ensure he was understood. 'But in many cases such fundamentalism results from other reasons such as economics.'

'Sir, how far have churches and personalities caused such fundamentalism? The Catholic Church itself has a tendency to overlord it over other Christian churches,' a girl to the right of the class said intelligently. She was a well-known critic of the school and its catholic origin and continued affiliation. This therefore didn't come as a surprise.

'As far as I know,' Mr. Maranga said to the attentive girls, 'The catholic church, and indeed other Christian churches have tended to personalize worship. The Church of England, for example, split from the Catholic Church because the then king of England had been denied the right to marry since the church did not approve of the marriage. The Catholic Church itself split from the Orthodox Church because the Roman Pope was too powerful and tended to lord it over the other four popes who originally formed the Holy See. That was a way of personalizing worship, don't you think?'

'And then there is this hypocrisy in churches today,' JMR said. 'Why is it that the government turns a blind eye to churches that exploit people's fear of the unknown? See how many churches in our country are simply ripping billions out of poor people?'

'What do you know o?' Chimaka said from her corner. 'You should see the type of Christianity we have in Nigeria. The things pastors make people especially women do! They are actually worse than wizards and witches.'

The class was in stitches. It was difficult to tell whether the humor was as a result of Chimaka's portrayal of Christianity in her country or because of her heavily accented English.

'Personally, I think worship should be regulated,' Mr Maranga quipped. 'It is wrong for any government to condone stealing from poor people by exploiting their belief or allowing the excesses that we see around us today. Many such governments are paying through the nose in the acts of terror we see around today.'

'It's Karma, I believe,' JMR said.

'Sir, are you sure we are still discussing History? I have a strange feeling that we are encroaching on the realm of the CRE teacher,' one of the girls said.

The others laughed as their History teacher smiled.

'That's the idea Carol,' the teacher said. 'All subjects tend to be integrated in some way. Indeed, there was once a time when students would learn generally without condemning ideas into this or that subject. During the early Greek and Roman kingdoms for example, students would be apprenticed to a teacher who would teach them what was then referred to as philosophy. It contained many of the other things you study in the different subjects you do today.'

The girls were so attentive that they did not hear the bell go and neither did the teacher. The teacher who was coming in next knocked at the door twice but all were too engrossed to hear. Five minutes or so after the bell, the door opened a crack and the light-skinned face of Mrs. Mantu, the Maths teacher, poked round, her eyes screwing as if to say that Mr. Maranga's History was not the only pebble on the beach. It was then that Mr. Maranga seemed to come out of the reverie into which History had confined him for the last fifty minutes or so.

'Sorry girls, we have to cut it short here. Remember to register for next week's visit to the museum in time,' he said as he gathered his books and went out.

Many girls were still smacking their lips at the prospect of the coming trip to the museum as Mr. Maranga went out. It was clear that Mrs. Mantu would have a rough time reorienting the students to algebra.

1: A Journey by Truck

The girls were out of luck, The History Club, that is. Their school bus was scheduled to ferry some teachers to a conference at the coastal town of Mombasa and therefore, the girls who were to visit the museum had no choice but to settle for Old Billy. At first, the girls were up in arms but they soon realised that they only had the Hobson's choice. Old Billy was actually an old Ford lorry which was as old as the school itself, probably as old as the hills too. It was now used to carry foodstuff from the local market near the school and sometimes to fetch firewood for the new energy saving *jikos* which had been erected in the sheltered open area outside the school kitchen. This made it difficult for the lorry to shake down a lingering jungle-and-farm-produce smell that stuck to it like a flea to a dog. The lorry driver's cabin was only large enough for the driver and the two teachers and therefore the fifty girls would have to settle for the back - a wooden affair covered by a corroded metal roof. The lower wooden sides rose a metre off the floor, then in place of windows, there was a half metre wire mesh between the wooden body and the rusty roof. Tough dull green tarpaulin which was used to cover these windows was normally rolled up or down to keep off the rain, wind or dust. It was an open secret that whenever girls found themselves forced to settle for that means of transport especially when visiting another school, they would alight outside the gate of the new school and walk in to save face. Many girls also saw Old Billy as a harbinger of bad luck; it had proven this true at a recent visit to St. Joseph's where the girls had been whipped eleven nil in a football match! Somebody had given Old Billy a lick and a promise in an attempt to improve the lorry's dowdy appearance.

The problem was that that morning, the girls had not been forewarned. As they emerged onto the parade ground where vehicles taking students out were normally parked, they were shocked to find Old Billy sweltering in the sun like an old cow fighting the tse tse in the heat of a March morning.

'Oh Lord in heaven,' Amy cried. 'Not Old Billy again!'

The lorry had been nicknamed Billy after its longest-serving driver. He had driven it for twenty nine years and the lorry had inherited his name after his death.

'Oh Allah the merciful,' cried Raj. 'I wonder what cock and bull story they have for us this time round.'

'We must protest to Mr. Maranga! Somebody is busy trying to kill the History Club,' Amy said.

'You are right on that one o,' Mak said coming on behind the other two girls. 'We need something with a womanly touch.' The last word came out 'torch' because Mak had a strong Nigerian accent which often left those not used to her laughing with amusement.

'You are out of luck girls,' Miss Lillian said as she brought up the rear. She was popular with the girls and many danced to her tune. 'The new school bus has been committed to take some teachers to a head's conference at the coast. Like it or lump it, this is the only means of transport we've got.'

'It's our bus,' Jennifer, a saved girl who was vice president of the History club said. 'It should be enjoyed by the students first. Everyone else should play second fiddle!'

'Besides, we should have been informed,' Amy said going with the flow, 'Forewarned is forearmed.'

'Mind your language young lady. Forearmed means you would have skipped the journey? My hands are tied for the principal insisted on a first come first served basis. Billy will have to do,' Mr. Maranga said coming to Teacher Lillian's rescue for Teacher Lillian had run out of words. 'The bus left on Sunday night and besides, you will all agree with me that Old Billy cannot in any way make it to Mombasa.'

The mood of the club was quickly going downhill.

'She doesn't look like she can make it anywhere o,' Mak said from behind the other girls causing a round of laughter.

'Maybe somebody's trying to ensure we are under the speed limit! Is this the only way they know how? Somebody should tell them their plan is not up to scratch!' Amy observed to another round of laughter. The girls were over the moon.

'Cut the raucous girls. The bottom line is that we've got to do with what we have. Besides, your spirits should be dancing at the prospect of what is to be found at the museum!' Mr. Maranga quipped.

It was probably this that calmed the girls down a little and lifted their spirits. They reluctantly began to see eye to eye with Mr. Maranga and grudgingly swallowed the bitter truth that they would have to settle for Old Billy. It was however agreed that they would be let down outside the gates of the museum. They could not dare enter the compound in the old thing. They climbed onto the back of the lorry tongue in cheek after the wooden door was lowered. The sitting area at the back had long wooden forms with the barest touch of cushion and the girls had to sit facing each other with their knees digging into each other or with their backs to each other, their heads knocking every time Old Billy went over a bump. Sitting this way, the wind drove into the passengers' ears too giving them motion sickness. When all of them were settled, the door was secured. The driver tried the lorry's engine which croaked like the clogged throat of a rheumatic buffalo, then went dead. He tried it several times - as the girls held their breath fearing they might have to alight and push - before it finally caught at probably the tenth try. He then stepped down severally on the accelerator and the lorry groaned then it was buried in a cloud of acrid diesel fumes from its exhaust pipe. The girls coughed inside the lorry as they quickly and desperately fanned themselves in a frantic attempt to keep off the acrid smoky fumes.

Finally, the old lorry stuttered forward, her underbelly creaking like an old castle threatening to come down as it went over the several bumps on the driveway to the gate. One of the girls started a chorus and the others took it up as the lorry went out of the school compound. It turned right and went down Factory Road that ran parallel to the school fence, before joining the road that led to town at the public library. Rather than turn right here and go through town, it turned left and went down towards Kiandutu slums as if conscious of shaming her human cargo if it took it through town. It drove down the road for two minutes before joining the Nairobi-Garissa highway where it turned right. The driver gunned down the engine but the old lorry could only do sixty kilometers an hour at its best – which felt a great punishment to her engine - and the girls were flabbergasted as they watched vehicles speed past them; the performance of every other vehicle was a notch above Old Billy. When they got to the Nairobi highway, Mak tried to lift the spirits of the girls by telling jokes to which the others quickly joined in.

'What horses go out at night?' she began.

'Night mares!' somebody said and the girls burst out into laughter.

'And where do ghosts go for their shopping?' Raj asked.

'In a ghost town!' somebody replied.

'Where does an elephant put his suitcases?'

'In his trunk!'

'What did the old flea say to the young one?'

'Do we walk or take a dog to town?'

'And what did the big chimney tell the small chimney?'

'You are too young to smoke!'

'Why did the first dog to go to space die?'

'It was dog-napped by aliens!'

The girls were having a field day as Billy laboured on. They saw the narrow road leading to St Joseph's High School flip by and many of them remembered a game they had had there recently. The results of the game had not initially been very nice and the consequences had nearly led Mrs. Mantu to quit teaching but Mak, Jenny and Julie Rosenthal had come to the teacher's – and to everybody's salvage. Eventually, the girls had won both a game and more importantly, their pride. Billy laboured on. He kept to the last lane and like a wary mouse caught up in the cat world, he managed to keep anonymous enough although this meant he had to contend with the many slow matatus which kept to that lane too. He labored past Ruiru town, KU to the right and Kahawa Barracks beyond.

It was a relief to the girls when a little over an hour later, the lorry turned into Forest Road and soon, they were relieved to see the blessed gates of the museum. The jokes had spiced the journey a little because with Old Billy, it would have turned just another run off the mill affair. It was just as good because by then, the girls were running out of steam. It was well past nine o'clock. Before anyone could remind the driver that he had promised to let the students off outside the gate, the lorry had driven into the compound and was reversing towards the east next to the Louis Leaky Auditorium to park smack dab in the middle of several shining school buses whose students had alighted and were milling confusedly all over the parking lot. They paused immediately to see what would come out of the new arrival. Avoiding their eyes, the driver came round and lowered the door again and the girls, most of whom were suffering from the Charley Horse had little choice but to alight and swallow their pride. They clicked their tongues at the driver but the driver looked away as if he was none the wiser; see no evil, hear no evil, he smiled bemused.

The teachers gathered the students a little way from their school bus.

'Hallo again girls,' Mr. Maranga began trying to strike the right note. 'It is a relief that our school bus has seen us safely here'.

'You can say that again!' somebody said amid laughter.

'Cut it out, please. Since we are already late, I'll plunge straight in without fanfare. We will begin with an initial guided tour of the western wing of the museum. That should take us an hour or so. After that, we will regroup here for refreshments which should take half an hour, then we will go back into the museum again. There will be another guided tour between eleven and one when we will go for lunch. Over lunch, we will discuss our next course of action.'

It was during the refreshment break later that Raj requested Mr. Maranga to let her rush to Westlands, a suburb to the west of the city, to see her parents who had an electronics establishment there. Naturally, she requested Mr. Maranga to let Amy, her bosom friend, accompany her there. Mr. Maranga reluctantly consented but emphasized that the two girls only had an hour.

2: A Trip to a Shopping Mall

It was therefore around eleven when Raj and Amy left the museum and walked down the road to the right of the gate of the museum so as to take a *matatu* at the bridge near The Aga Khan Nursery School. Ten minutes later, the *matatu* deposited them at a roundabout near Sarit Centre from where they walked to the Westgate Shopping Mall.

'This is Amy,' Raj told her excited parents proudly when they got to the mall. 'She is my best friend in school although she is in Form One.' She went ahead to tell them how they had met earlier in the year and how she had 'mothered' her friend for the nearly eight months Amy had been at St. Mary's.

'It's like an eight-month pregnancy,' Raj observed.

'And it is one month before I am born!' Amy concurred.

'You girls must be hungry,' Raj's mother said as she escorted the girls to a café on the first floor of the expansive shopping mall.

'You can say that again. I'm starved,' Raj said smiling at her mother. 'You wouldn't believe the stuff they feed us at school.'

'School in not exactly a holiday camp,' her mother responded good-naturedly. 'It's meant to teach you that life isn't a bed of roses.'

'Not the way they do it at St. Mary's mom,' Raj said defensively. 'You would think we are being trained for desert combat in Iraq or Afghanistan!'

'Ok, ok. You know what, hardships in school are often a blessing in disguise but you only come to realize that long after you've hit the road in real life. For now, I'm ready to accept anything you say as long as you promise to take a good meal, then go right back to the museum. Remember, you should make hay while the sun shines.' Her mom said as she led the two girls to the stairs. 'Somebody once said that after a good meal, one can forgive anybody – even one's own relatives and apparently errant school masters.'

'That was Oscar Wilde,' Amy whispered to her friend who winked at her. She saw that Raj's attempt to paint St. M in bad light to her mother was nothing doing. The old lady was no spring chicken; she could not be easily fooled.

'Sure we will mum,' Raj said, 'a good meal is worth fighting for and I think we've just earned one. But it is true. The taste buds of whoever does food tasting at school must be as dead as the wholesale district on a Sunday.'

Raj blew her cheeks feeling that as long as her mother was ready to pick up the tab, she would agree with her. Looking at mother and daughter, Amy found herself thinking that the apple never falls far from the tree. Raj's mother looked ready to bend over backwards for her daughter, just like Raj did for her at school. It appeared that humility ran in the family.

At the head of the spiral staircase, they emerged onto a landing with a corridor that stretched straight ahead to the left. Along the corridor, there were different businesses to their left; jewelers, several clothes stores and a bakery whose aroma of doughnuts and roast peanuts escorted them down the corridor. They did not notice the excited dark man who beamed when he saw their uniforms and tried to wave at them. To their right was an open area through which they could see the escalators, the business stands downstairs and on the opposite side of the building. The café was at the corner at the end of the corridor beyond one of the escalators that led to the lower floor. It had shiny aluminum tables and similar seats which were fixed to the marble floor leaving little space for maneuver. Businesses here were going great guns.

The café turned out to be a haven for Indian food though the girls only settled for Indian spiced chicken with spinach and chips. It was flavoured with herbs and hot pepper and Amy had to drink like a fish as they ate although she had already been introduced to Indian recipes when she and Raj visited Dhrupti's parents earlier in the year. She insisted on taking what her friend and her mother had opted for. Raj looked at her as if to say 'eat, drink and be merry for tomorrow we die; this is no dry run.' All the same, the food was finger licking good and the girls wondered whether to ask for a doggie bag. It was probably why the café was as busy as a beehive; after all, nothing succeeds like success. Uncannily, Amy felt like she was eating with two mothers at the same time. The girls washed the food down with a lot of cocktailed fresh juice as they told the beaming rosy-cheeked Indian woman girl stories of school. Her face, which dimpled as she smiled, had a red spot on the forehead which proclaimed she was Hindu. Her shiny jet-black hair parted in the middle of her head to leave a pale groove. It was tied behind her head with something Amy couldn't see to flow down her back in two pony tails.

After the meal, Raj told her mother that her school shopping was running down and needed replenishing. Her mother gave her some money and the two girls took the escalator to the supermarket downstairs as Raj's mother went away and the two girls promised to shop quickly and meet her at her business perch. When they got downstairs, the girls walked to their right and entered a large supermarket which occupied two floors on one end of the shopping mall. Soft music played from some unseen speakers; at the moment, Air Supply's *Lost in Love*, issued from somewhere high above them. Raj who had shopped in the supermarket several times before led her friend past the various shelves packed high with tantalizing goods as she sought out what she wanted. Feeling luxuriant, she bought two cones of ice cream and the two lapped at it as they sorted out what to buy. They expected to be in the dog house with Mr. Maranga by the time they returned for there was no way they would make it back to the museum in time.

'Don't you think you need a list of sorts?' Amy asked her friend noticing from the price tags that she had to part with an arm and a leg. 'At this rate you'll turn your mum as poor as a church mouse. Money doesn't grow on trees, you know.'

'I can't help it. We are running against the clock; we have under half-an-hour to make it back to the museum, which I needn't say, will be a tall order.'

'I think we took too long with that chicken. All the same, you might find that you bought little of what you required once you get back to school. Haste makes waste, you know.'

'As long as I have soap and toothpaste I think I'll survive,' Raj joked. None of what she had mentioned was in the shopping basket yet. Neither of the two girls however knew that their plans would soon fall by the wayside.

It was while they were sorting out some tins of jam that they heard a commotion outside the mall. There were shouts of 'Everybody on the floor! Everybody down' which were followed by gunshots, then loud screams. The two girls instinctively crouched but a split-second later, they heard more gunshots followed by wild screams. They rose as one and ran towards the end of the supermarket where the throng of scared shoppers seemed to be heading.

'There is a back exit somewhere here,' somebody shouted.

'What's happening over there?' another raised voice queried.

'Robbers I suppose,' the first voice replied.

Further ahead, the two girls joined the horde as people – shoppers, workers at the supermarket and security people – crowded around a small exit which had been opened at the back, running as if everybody had gone nuts. Soon, they came out onto a large open area which was used as a loading and unloading zone for goods brought to the supermarket as well as for the trash taken out of it. Several containerized Lorries with the supermarket's name and logo splashed across their white sides were packed outside. Two of them appeared to have been loading cartons of trash before the commotion. Their rear doors were gaping open like the mouths of mysterious caves and parking cartons, nylon wrapping paper, strips of plastic tie-ons and a lot of other trash was splattered on the ground. The rest of the backyard was nothing to write home about. Further ahead, there was a large dark-blue wrought iron gate within which there was a smaller open gate. The crowd of people hurried towards it. The two girls were still caught among the multitude and they were pushed by the throng as everybody made for the gate.

However, after several people had gone out of the gate, there was renewed gunfire from beyond the gate and people hastily turned back and headed the way they had come. Amy was just in time to see a man in dark clothes and a chequered red-and-white Arafat turban wound round his head come in. He had an ugly-looking rifle in his hands and as the people ran away, he started shooting into the crowd! The mob found itself between a rock and a hard place. People trampled over each other in the ensuing panic as they fought for the only door back into the supermarket. The two girls were not only lucky enough to go through the door but they also somehow kept together. They followed a group of women with children as they ran to the right of the supermarket's ground floor. At the end of the line of high shelves, they suddenly came on to the meat section. It had large freezers with glass tops that let customers view the wares inside. The two girls followed the women as some flew over the counters while others went round the freezers. They all took cover behind the counters and waited out of sight keeping their fingers crossed. Every now and then, a staccato burst of gunfire punctuated the general screams and the chaos which the formerly serene supermarket had become but the shooters were nowhere in sight.

'What the hell is going on?' a woman who sounded quite in the dark wondered aloud. She sounded ready to run at the drop of a hat.

'Thieves, most likely. Many are all bark and no bite; if we stay put, they should leave once they clear the tills. That's where the gunfire seems to be coming from,' another replied skeptically.

The women held their children down and covered their ears to stop the gunfire from scaring them. The very small children cried into their mother's hands as their mouths were covered to stop them from drawing attention to their hide out. It was sometime before the hiding group realized that there was more to the whole thing than met the eye. Even when the noise lessened somewhat, sporadic gunshots followed by screams of pain continued punctuating the silence every now and then. It became clear that whoever was shooting wasn't going away; they were interested in more than money. It was then that most people in the hiding crowd realized that the shooters might have a lot up their sleeve.

'I see one of them,' one of the children whispered.

Amy who was shaking like a leaf in an April storm turned slowly and looked down the space between two freezers. At the end of the long corridor between two shelves, she could see a man in a blue long-sleeved shirt; he was holding some kind of nasty-looking rifle which was aimed somewhere ahead of him. He walked slowly throwing eagle eyes here and there as if searching for something, then stopped. He then looked up as if trying to see where the security cameras were. Near where he stood, Amy could make out a male employee cowering under a till, out of sight. The gunman aimed his gun somewhere above him then shot several rounds as he cried in a guttural tongue. Something crashed above him before shards of glass and plastic showered like confetti on to the floor. Both the lights and the music went intermittently on and off, then steadied again. The man crouching under the till must have made some noise for the gunman who was walking away suddenly stopped and turned round. He crouched on one knee as he looked under the tills and saw the man who was hiding there. He shot twice and the man whimpered in pain. He crawled out of his hiding place then tried to stand as he raised his hands in surrender but fell back to the floor as if on legs of jelly. The gunman walked casually towards him and stood above him with his gun trained on the man's head.

'Allahu akubar!' he shouted, then shot the man who was writhing on the floor twice in the head at close range. The man spread out like a drop of oil in a pool, then went still. Amy wretched as she quickly turned away. She began to pray. Everything had suddenly fallen into place.

'Good Lord! These aren't thugs,' she whispered to Raj who was lying as flat as a pancake on the floor next to her. 'These Arafat turbans do not look interested in any money.'

'Hold tight and make sure you're out of sight,' her friend whispered back.

They lay as still as tree stumps for some time as intermittent gunfire continued inside and outside the supermarket.

'We need to hide further away,' Amy whispered turning to the woman next to her.

'Now you are talking,' the woman who appeared to have the nuts and bolts of a crisis at her finger tips said, 'We must protect the children; they are the future that can change this crazy world.'

There were three women, a man and six children. One white woman in a rose-red dress had a girl and a boy about six and ten years of age. There was another woman with oriental features who had a child of about a year in her arms. There was a south Asian couple who looked Malaysian or Pilipino who had a girl of about three and there were two girls of about three and four who had been separated from their mother as people ran helter-skelter for cover.

'These people aren't going away and if we sit here, I'm sure we are sitting ducks, perish the thought,' Raj said agreeing with Amy. 'We need to at least keep the children out of sight.'

'What can we do?' the Asian woman whispered.

'Hide the children between the freezers over there,' Amy suggested nodding at two big freezers behind her with space enough between them to squeeze the children in.

The women concurred and the children were quietly directed to crawl and hide there. Once in place, two women crawled over and squatted in front of them covering them as well as they could. The Asian man rose on one knee and examined the supermarket through the misty glass of the meat display freezers. All seemed quiet. Stevie Wonder's *I Just Called to Say I Love You* began playing in some speakers high above the scared group. Suddenly, the man jumped back as a crowd of about

a dozen people or so came rushing where the group was hiding and crouched behind the meat freezers with them. That seemed to attract the attention of one of the gunmen and they heard deliberate footsteps running their way.

'I see him! I see him, he's coming this way,' a girl whispered desperately.

Amy thought the fearful girl was crying wolf until she saw the man get into and out of view herself. Then peripatetic footsteps continued wandering about beyond the meat display counters. In spite of what was going on, Amy didn't think that the gunmen would deliberately kill innocent women and children. She thought that the worst that could happen was that they would be kept hostage until the gunmen were granted whatever they sought. She was as wrong as the weatherman. The thought had hardly taken proper perspective when the footsteps she had heard stopped a little way from where they were. Immediately after, there was a continuous volley of gunfire that blasted through the counters and the freezers showering them with shards of plastic, wood and glass. The shooting went on for about twenty seconds amid frantic screams of pain and panic. Amy sat tight and prayed as the Indian man who had been keeping watch earlier was lifted up in the air by bullets before he fell on her dead as a doornail. She realized he was dead when he went still as blood that poured out of him soaked her clothes.

'Allahu akbar!' the gunman shouted. 'Death to all infidels.'

'Have mercy! Kill us but let the innocent children go,' a woman cried.

'We will kill every infidel whether they are adults or children, anyone who tries to pervert the course of justice,' the gunman who was clearly a loose cannon shouted in broken English. He looked like he was ready to go the whole hog now that he was already in the thick of it. It looked like it was in for a penny, in for a pound. Besides, he looked like he had an axe to grind with everybody. The anger in his voice warned the woman to keep quiet though she was in bad shape. In the silence that followed, which was only punctuated by the whimpering of children, another pair of footsteps approached. Stevie Wonder's voice which had replaced the volley of bullets continued in the background.

'No Omar, we won't kill innocent women or children, not those with whom we have no quarrel,' another voice said. 'We must put things in their right perspective. It is an ill wind that blows no one any good.'

Raj stole a look and saw the new gunman nearby. He was tall, about six-foot two, dressed in a neat shirt and casual trousers under which Nike sport shoes protruded. On his head was the tell-tale red-and-white turban which partly covered his face to leave out only the nose and two black eyes hard as granite. He had a nasty looking gun trained on the group of bloody, crying victims of his colleague. Something in Raj stirred and she knelt facing the two gunmen who immediately trained their guns on her as she faced them.

'You are unholy,' she told them taking her courage in both hands. 'Do not kill in the name of Allah! Islam is holy and has no place for people whose hands are bloodied with innocent blood of children.'

Whoever said that fear is the father of courage and the mother of safety? Amy wondered as she looked at her bold friend and tagged at her skirt to silence her. It was clear that everyone else was burying their heads in the sand and wishing the problem away.

'Shut up! What do you know about Islam infidel?' the first gunman shouted wildly as he trained his gun firmly on the short stout Indian girl. His colleague pushed the barrel slowly away. The white woman next to Raj spoke.

'Let the children go. They are simply caught in the crossfire. They should not suffer for things they know nothing about.'

The second gunman seemed to consider that. He held the elbow of his fuming colleague and edged him away. More gunfire reports came from the direction in which they had gone.

'Are you hurt?' Raj asked Amy as she lay next to her flat as a floorboard.

'No…I…I don't think so,' Amy whispered as she crawled from under the body of the man who had fallen on her.

She raised her head carefully and looked around as if trying to decide the best way to pick up the pieces. There was blood everywhere she looked. This was no dog and pony show – the terrorists meant business. People were groaning around her and in the crimson environment, it was difficult to tell who was dead and who wasn't. Beyond the freezers, behind which they lay, she could see several still bodies on the floor. The way they lay and the blood surrounding them told horror stories of how they had met with death.

'Stop crying or they will come back,' the white woman who had spoken to the gunmen said to a small boy who had been shot through the thigh. He cried silently as he regarded the bloody motionless bodies of his parents who had been shot at close range. The white woman stretched out and squeezed his hand as she tried to stem his bleeding with the other hand.

'Hold my hand and don't let go,' she said in heavily accented English. 'Shut your eyes and do not raise your head even if you hear them coming back.' The boy obeyed her commands but continued to whimper in pain.

Presently, the second terrorist returned. He had a bandage roll with him and he tossed it at the white woman.

'Dress him up,' he rasped. 'What has happened was unfortunate. We are not monsters out to kill innocent women and children. We also have no quarrel with other Muslims but they will have to cooperate.'

Nobody apart from the white woman moved. She too had been shot in the hip and blood trickled down her right leg as she rose and mechanically unwound the roll of bandage and tried to stem the small boy's bleeding as much as she could. The terrorist's statuesque face looked on. When the white woman was through, the terrorist moved back a little and trained his gun on the group.

'We will let any children still alive out of here,' he said but his announcement was taken with a grain of salt. His impassive face and drug-laced eyes seemed to tell a different story. He seemed momentarily indecisive.

High up above somewhere, some cheery music continued playing. Some mechanical fault made the power and the music go on and off. The whirring of the meat freezers also went on and off in some uncanny rhythm. Nobody else moved. After what seemed an eternity, the white woman stood slowly. She was shaking like a leaf in a blizzard and looking at her, Amy thought she would put all of them in renewed danger. The pointed barrel of the terrorist's gun followed her up as she rose. She had the makings of the Biblical David who stood up against Goliath.

'Please,' she addressed the terrorist going all out to appeal to his sense of humanity. 'There are several children cowering here. Please let them go.'

'Only the very young,' the terrorist said. 'Everyone else, you included stays unless you want to be in a pretty pickle soon.'

The ice did not once leave his voice. He stood casually on the tiled blood-soaked floor looking over the distressed group as if he was overseeing a pass out of fellow terrorists. The white woman began gathering the children who were still alive and could move. There were nine in all. Nobody else, including their parents dared move. It looked like the terrorist could change his mind before the ink was dry.

'We are not the monsters you think we are,' the terrorist repeated, addressing the white woman. She did not once look up to his face as she gathered the distressed children.

'These ones can't walk,' she told the terrorist. 'Can I put them on a trolley?'

The terrorist nodded seeming to have a change of heart. The white woman limped down the corridor and came back pushing a large wire mesh shopping trolley. From the way the terrorist talked, he sounded like the woman had touched a soft spot in him, giving him a sense of second thought.

'Where do you hail?' he asked her as she went about putting three children who had been badly injured onto the trolley.

Raj rose carefully and looking at the terrorist to see whether he'd object, she went over to help her. The girl was full of the milk of human kindness.

'Germany,' the white woman said in heavily accented English.

'We do not want to hurt you foreigners,' the terrorist said. 'You must forgive us. You only happened to be collateral damage.'

The woman did not respond as the terrorist had expected her to. She had finished putting the three children onto the trolley and appeared to be waiting for permission to take them away.

'We are only giving these people a stern warning that if they kill us in our homeland, we will pursue them here and kill them too, get the picture?' the terrorist continued picking up steam.

He seemed eager to be understood and to appear to apologize for what his thoughtless colleague had done. It looked too, like there was something he hadn't been told by whoever had sent him. The white woman stood there holding onto two children and looking at the floor. The terrorist motioned to Raj to help the white woman push the trolley and the three accompanied the children as they hobbled down the corridor towards the entrance of the supermarket. Chris De Barge's *Lady in Red* began playing above them. One of the wounded boys was so weak that he could hardly walk. He had been weakened by both blood loss and the over half-an-hour of distressful crouching near a cold freezer and was beginning to show a labored breathing. The terrorist asked the white woman to carry him. The woman and the eight children walked down the corridor towards the tills where number crunchers had been busy about an hour earlier. They walked as if on feet of clay, then went round the tills towards the entrance. Raj pushed the trolley beside them. The terrorist seemed cautious and he threw his eyes here and there to ensure that no one else was about. Once round the tills, he beckoned the teenage girl with the muzzle of his gun and she fell back. The white woman looked at the terrorist uncomprehendingly, then went over to push the trolley which carried the three injured children. The terrorist and the teenage girl stood there as they watched the white woman and the children go out of the entrance, then the terrorist nudged the girl back into the supermarket and followed her, his gun trained on the small of her back.

Before they got back to the meat section of the supermarket, sporadic gunfire erupted outside the mall. It sounded like it was coming from the main entrance through which the white woman and the children had just exited a moment before. The second terrorist was already shepherding the group that had been left behind out of the meat section.

'Up! Up!' he commanded putting them through the mill as he trained his gun on them, then guarded them down the corridor towards the rear of the supermarket.

'Up the stairs quickly!' he commanded as they came to a spiral staircase at the rear of the supermarket. They joined another crowd of shoppers and employees of the supermarket and crowded at a short flight of stairs with another terrorist who was trying to get them up to the first floor following them closely behind. Shoppers who had abandoned their bags ran up the stairs holding small children and fighting to get away at the same time. Instinctively, Raj reached out and held her friend's hand as they scrambled among the crowd and were literally carried up the stairs by the frightened throng. She had a strong feeling this would turn a bad hair day.

3: An Afternoon Ordeal

It was sometime before the History Club realized what had befallen two of their colleagues. It began by Mak's wondering aloud why the two girls had taken so long to get to Westlands and back; and nobody knew better than her because her parents were business people there too. Over an hour after the two girls had left, the teachers got wind of the fact that there had been a terrorist attack at the Westgate Mall in Nairobi's Westlands area. It was nearly one o'clock and the news of the terrorist attack was all over the media. A hasty conference was called, first between the two teachers and the driver and then for the whole History Club after it had been confirmed from Mak that indeed Raj's parents had businesses at the mall and that by all looks and intents, the girls had been caught up in the attack when it happened at around half past eleven that morning. From the look of things, they were still holed up there.

'Girls,' Mr. Maranga began, 'I'd hate to be the herald of bad news but it appears that two of our colleagues are likely to have been caught up in a nasty situation in Nairobi's Westlands area.'

There were murmured conversations because many of the girls had not even noticed that Raj and Amy were missing. It was clear too that Mr. Maranga was slightly bending the truth.

'Miss Manji and her friend Amy left us to visit Miss Manji's parents briefly this morning and we were hoping they would be back by half past eleven,' teacher Lillian filled in on Mr. Maranga's scattered thoughts.

'Chimaka here tells me that the very place they were headed for is the same that has been attacked by terrorists. Chimaka, can you please shed light on the issue?' Mr. Maranga said nodding at the Nigerian girl every student called Mak.

'Yeah,' the girl spoke up. 'My parents have a jewelers shop in the same mall and Raj and I have visited her parents severally. They have a mobile phone and computer establishment at the same mall. However, I'm not sure my parents are there right now.'

'We've been holding our breath hoping time will prove our fears unfounded but now with this knowledge,' Mr. Maranga said after some time, 'we can only assume the worst.'

'We have already called St. Mary's and got the phone number of Manji's parents but the number goes unanswered,' Miss Lillian said. 'As much as we cannot go to the mall itself, we have little choice but to suspend the afternoon session and decide what to do for the two girls as we hope for the best,' Mr. Maranga said. 'Meanwhile, the driver and I will go out and shop for some food. Even in such grim circumstances, some immediate needs must be addressed to give us energy for the task ahead.'

After a few deliberations, it was decided that the whole group could walk to the Ngara area and look for a fast food joint rather than have the teacher ferrying bags of chips to them. Many of the girls were grateful for this distraction for it kept them from thinking about what their friends might have been going through at that very moment. What kept many calm was the fact that it had not been ascertained whether their friends were still in the mall or the exact nature of danger they were in, otherwise the girls could easily have become hysterical. All the same, lunch was a dreary affair and by two in the afternoon, the majority of the girls were for sitting tight until their colleagues were found. It was Mak, in fact, who eventually came up with the idea of going as close to the mall as they dared and keeping vigil until the two girls were found – in spite of Mr. Maranga's warning that it is curiosity that killed the cat. So at around two thirty, the old school bus drove out of the museum compound, crossed over the road to town and took the fly over which would take it all the way to the Consolata Shrine on Waiyaki Way where it would double back, come down the way towards town before joining Ojijo Road at the flyover opposite the museum. Ojijo road would take them to Parklands and to the police station there from where the teachers would make up their minds what should be done next.

At the Parklands Police Station, the teachers made a formal report about the missing girls as the rest of the girls waited outside and kept their fingers crossed.

'We ought to form some sort of support group to lend a hand to the victims as we await the news of Raj and Amy. We can't sit fiddling while Rome burns,' Mak who was head and shoulders above the others opined. She often ran rings around other girls when it came to thinking quickly.

'That's a helluva idea,' Jenny said. 'It ought to keep our minds occupied enough to prevent us from going crazy as we wait. And the time will be spent in a worthwhile manner. This is as good a time to send up a trial balloon as any.'

'But we should let the teachers make the decisions themselves. It is not just about getting a piece of the action,' an albino girl called Rehema objected.

'Those teachers are so stressed I'm sure they can't think straight right now. And if I was in their shoes, I'd vote for going back to school straight away. I'm not sure whether there is anyone here willing to go back to school and leave our colleagues in trouble?' JMR queried.

'We can't.' the girls chorused. 'No one is so crazy as to vote with their feet!' Nasibo added. Everybody understood for she was the closest friend to Raj and Amy.

'Then all we have to do is inform Mr. Maranga,' Mak said. 'Can we think of how to go about things as we wait for the teachers – some back of the envelop calculation of what is required?'

'The first thing we need is a tent,' another girl, Julie Marie Rosenthal, who the girls variously called Marie Rose, JR or JMR said. She was the deputy secretary of the Girl Guides back at St. Mary's and therefore this did not come as a surprise to the other girls – she knew such things like the back of her hand and was already on auto pilot.

'And some tables and chairs,' Jane Rose offered.

'Any suggestions?' Mak asked looking around at the assembled group.

'Our best bet would be a school. Which ones are near here?' Marie Rose asked. 'Or colleges.'

'The two Parklands secondary schools are around here but I'm not sure where,' Rehema said. 'There's also Kenya High and Nairobi school due west.'

'The Parklands schools should be the nearest but I think both are day schools,' another girl said. 'They may not be blessed with some of the facilities you could find in a boarding school. There are also Jamhuri and Ngara Girls in the Ngara area near town.'

'That means we will need four pairs of girls to visit these schools and find out. Can we have four pairs of girls who know where these schools are?'

There were murmurs akin to the waves on the shore as the wind dies away and within a short time, four pairs of girls were found.

'We won't need all those tents, so we will have to visit the schools one by one,' Mak who had an old head on young shoulders took charge. 'If we can't get help from the nearest, then we will try the ones further away.'

'Our best bet would be to have the teachers call those schools before anyone visits them. What we should look for are the telephone numbers of the suggested schools,' Marie Rose said intelligently.

Everyone agreed, some of them going along for the ride. A hasty conference was called between groups of girls as they tried to come up with the telephone numbers. Three girls were sent to consult the telephone directory at the police station.

By the time the teachers returned, the girls had done most of the ground work and a preliminary plan of action had taken shape. Like they say, a job is only that which hasn't cropped up. The teachers had little choice but to go along with the girls whose determination left no room for argument. They called St. Mary's and informed Ms. Konga, the Principal, who had earlier been for the girls being driven out of the city as quickly as possible. Marie Rose talked to the Principal herself as Mr. Maranga convinced her that the girls had refused to budge and that he personally thought their idea of trying to help in some way was a very noble one. Somebody suggested that they should come up with a formal name of address in case they wanted to contact the press. It was agreed that they could settle for 'St Maryan Rescue Team'. Mr. Maranga's phone became the group's hot line. It was a complete about turn on Mr. Maranga's part because under normal circumstances, he'd have been the first person to send the girls about their businesses.

It must have been the lingering of the school bus at the police station that attracted the attention of the Deputy OCS, a big light-skinned Swahili lady with the impossible name of 'Amina Jumamosi'. She came over to enquire whether the school party had received any attention from her officers.

'The girls have come up with the idea of helping victims of that attack,' Mr. Maranga explained. 'We've just been trying to iron out the details of how we should go about it.'

'It is very thoughtful of you girls to chip in. There are so many lives at stake and we really need citizens like you. Desperate times call for desperate measures,' the police officer said.

She was in a dark grey uniform with several shining brass medals jingling on the right side of her broad chest as she talked. A blue name tag on the left identified her and her rank. Two sharp eyes that missed nothing considered the group from under the peak of her cap. Somehow, she still managed to remain feminine and a motherly feeling exuded from her in spite of her aura of authority. Though her face remained expressionless, she had a way of looking at you with her lips slightly parted revealing the edge of her lower teeth which distanced her a little from the normal callousness of the ordinary police officer on the beat. The girls could see she never missed a trick.

'You will need some ground from which to conduct such an operation; this isn't exactly a piece of cake,' she said. It sounded uncanny to refer to the simple rescue the girls had in mind as an operation.

'Sure,' Mr. Maranga quipped. He seemed to have gotten over the initial scare and though he didn't say it, you could tell he was glad for what the girls were doing. His frown had lessened somewhat and his right hand which had constantly been pulling at his three day stubble thoughtfully had found something better to do. He appeared to let go his fixed ways.

'Then I suggest that we look for a place here where we can house you,' the police officer said simply as she looked around the parking lot of the police station.

Carcasses of vehicles salvaged from accidents were all over the parking lot to the left side of the driveway. The main offices were at the edge of the driveway with toilet facilities to the right of the main building. Behind the main building were living quarters for the officers which were accessed via an open space to the left between the edge of the main offices and its perimeter fence. The space was narrow for the skeletons of wrecked vehicles stretched all the way to the back in order to leave enough space for the parking. The Deputy OCS elected for settling the St Maryan Rescue Team somewhere there, away from the hubbub of the police station's front office which was already a beehive of activity. A number of officers were called to make space large enough for the girls to pitch a tent. They had to push several shells of vehicles for the available space wasn't enough to swing a cat but by and by, they managed to create some space big enough to stretch.

By the time this space was cleared, it was already five. A tent and scant furniture had already been found and the girls quickly established their temporary headquarters. Amina, the deputy OCS, supervised every little detail of the operation between coordinating her own office and gathering news of the Westgate attack where her boss was.

'This is one of the nearest police stations to the Westgate Mall,' she told the girls. 'In fact, we are only a stone's throw away. As a result, most of my officers rushed there when we heard of the initial attack.'

'Oh sorry,' Miss Lillian said. 'We didn't know we were adding to your headache.'

'No don't mention it. Here in the city we are used to operating on a skeleton staff although we haven't had to be this stretched before.'

'Anything we can do to help, please let us know,' Mr. Maranga said. 'We have to see that we compensate you somehow.'

'Why don't we begin by seeing how we can make tea for the officers rescuing the victims?' Marie Rose suggested.

'That is a brilliant idea. You are the silver lining of this cloud!' Amina said and patted her on the shoulder. 'We can begin by collecting donations from our own staff here. They are very ready to help.'

'Chima,' Teacher Lillian addressed Mak whose name she often abbreviated that way, 'Get us three good girls who can see to that.'

Mak left forthwith and soon returned with three girls. The three left for the police lines behind the main offices with Amina. Ten minutes later, they returned with a charcoal stove, tea leaves, coffee, milk and other foodstuff. They also had a small plastic basket in which there were bank notes and coins which they handed to Teacher Lillian. The girls set forth making coffee to be taken to the officers who were conducting the rescue. A rumour had spread within the police station that there were students there trying to help the victims of the Westgate attack. Soon, even ordinary visitors to the police station began passing by to enquire what kind of help the girls needed. Donations began to pile as people brought money, foodstuff, blankets and drinking water. Indian businessmen drove into the police station in droves with mobile toilet and bathing facilities and other emergency stuff and the girls were glad for they were beginning to need such.

'Oh, that was quite a relief,' Mak said as she returned from the new toilet facilities.

'Yeah we can tell,' Jane Rose said from behind a group of girls with whom she was busy cutting up cabbage on a makeshift table. 'Your stomach was beginning to sound like the initial symptoms of a thunderstorm!' Many who heard fell into fits of laughter.

'Hear the pot calling the kettle black! Better me,' Mak responded. 'You better hurry there yourself. I've just heard someone wonder aloud whether the sewers have opened up or something!'

More laughter followed.

'That's for sure,' someone else said. 'I was beginning to wonder too whether fresh cabbage rots immediately after meeting some kind of hands. Now I know where the stench is coming from!' A burst of prolonged laughter crowned that.

'Hey girls,' Teacher Lillian said as she came from behind the school lorry. 'We are officially supposed to be in mourning. It is beginning to look like we are here for fun.' She said jokingly.

'Let the girls be,' Mr. Maranga said. He sat a little away from the group of busy girls, a disposable cup of very black coffee in his hand. 'We have already asked for too much from them. I'm beginning to wonder where I would have been suppose this was some other club.'

'That's a compliment girls!' Teacher Lillian said to the silence that followed. A number of girls 'mmmhed' in appreciation.

'The credit goes to Mak and Marie Rose here. They came up with this idea,' Rehema said.

'The credit goes to you all,' Teacher Lillian said. 'It is quite rare to see a group of girls thinking ahead of their teachers. That is really first class.'

'And defying Ms. Konga in the process,' somebody said. That was greeted with a bout of laughter.

'I'm very glad girls for this initiative. This isn't exactly child's play. The next time something happens when you are on your own I don't think I'll cry myself to grief wondering what will become of you,' Mr. Maranga said.

'Thank you sir,' Mak said. 'It might help you a little to know that what you see in us results from the trust we have in you. I'm not sure we would think this straight with someone else other than you and Teacher Lillian here. We are your mirror images.'

'And that is because we have a history of experience!' Teacher Lillian punned.

Everybody welcomed that with another burst of laughter. She often helped to keep the girls in line feeling that they could easily run riot with Mr. Maranga's free rein.

'Mind your Ps and Qs and give it a rest girls,' Mr. Maranga said feeling that some girls were over stepping the mark especially by criticizing their Principal in front of their teachers. 'Let's focus on how to help those two girls. It is clear those terrorists will give us a run for our money – and we need to get some work done; there's a certain feeling of too many chiefs and not enough Indians here!'

By six o'clock that evening, rescue operations had gone into overdrive and the police Land Cruiser's regular trips to the Westgate site had become an accepted phenomenon. The girls were busy making tea, coffee and sandwiches out of the supplies that came from well-wishers. The police vehicle itself brought in more supplies especially foodstuff that had been donated by market people in the city. A lot of donations had been taken to the Central Police Station but since there was no one there to turn them into an edible meal, they were turned over to the girls at the Parklands Police station. It became clear that the news of what the girls were doing had spread to other parts of the city. Just before dark, the girls were surprised to see the press led by an old girl at St Mary's who showed off in front of other journalists because girls from her old school had led such an initiative way before the Red Cross and St. John's Ambulance.

Raj's parents had been rescued from the mall although there was no sign of their daughter or her friend. Soon, the couple was led to Parklands Police Station where it immediately became part of the St. Maryan Rescue Team. The girls were also surprised to learn that the couple's home was only a stone's throw away but Raj's father firmly declared that he and his wife would stay put until news of the two girls was forthcoming.

By seven o'clock that evening, other tents had been erected adjacent to the first and the girls were busy seeing to food and hot drinks both for the rescuers and for those who, like them, had opted to keep vigil until the situation at the Westgate Mall was dissolved. It had already become clear that it was a terrorist attack and with news of the attackers taking hostages, everyone assumed the worst and settled down to a long prayerful wait.

4: All's not well...

When they got to the landing of the spiral staircase, Amy smelt a rat. She realized why the terrorists had chosen the spot. From here, one had a view as clear as solid sunshine. She could see the entire lower floor of the supermarket and it occurred to her that from here, the terrorists could easily monitor what was happening below. They could effortlessly see anyone who tried to come in through the main entrance as well as monitor any movements of anyone holed up on the floor below them. It was from here that she saw the real extent of the disaster. Bodies lay strewn out on the lower floor all the way to the entrance like a macabre scene from *Black Hawk Down*. Two terrorists were walking down the corridors between shelves looking for anyone who was alive. Every time one came upon somebody, he would stop and shout something in Arabic. Depending on the response the terrorist got, the victim would either be shot through the head or be told to rise and leave the supermarket. Apparently, the terrorists were more interested in taking women and children hostage. Those they found in the lower floor were shepherded to the upper floor to join the other group of hostages. Amy noticed too that at the back of the supermarket, there was some kind of store where the terrorists went to pray. They had a mat spread out on the floor on which they prayed in turns as one of them kept guard.

It appeared that there were only four of them, at least the ones that Amy had seen. There was the harsh one dressed in a blue shirt and casual trousers, then there was another slim one who wore blue jeans under a pink long-sleeved shirt. The one who had come to their rescue down stairs who Amy came to label 'the good hearted one' was in a spotless white shirt and black-grey trousers. The last of them was in desert camouflage trousers under a black jacket. This one spent most of his time walking the supermarket and Amy rarely saw him. He might have been wounded although he tried not to show it because there was a fresh smudge of blood on the lower left leg of his trousers; he also appeared to limp involuntarily. The good hearted one who looked the most level-headed appeared to be their commander. He looked more intelligent than the others who often appeared unable to come to decisions and to defer to him. They also appeared more irrational and unlike him, the other three were quite irascible. All of them appeared to use the turbans to avoid identification for when they went to the lower floor, they lowered the face covering and walked about freely. They however took care to pull them above the nose, disguising themselves like bunglers on the prowl, when they came up to their hostages on the upper floor. They had several mobile phones and walkie-talkies through which they appeared to communicate to each other and to other people outside the mall. On their waists were belts with small canvas bags hooked to them. From there, they regularly replenished their rifles. Each had at least one other rifle slung down his back. Amy also saw what she thought were grenades hooked to their belts.

The harsh terrorist kept guard over them when the good one went downstairs. He appeared to make a real effort to avoid looking at the group of hostages and spent the time pacing the length of the long corridor overlooking the lower floor. His granite hard eyes were trained somewhere in the lower floor and he only seemed to be conscious of their presence from the fact that he had left them there and none had so far made any attempt to escape. Amy and her friend were as quiet as two kittens as they watched the movement of the other terrorists on the lower floor. The terrorists scanned the premises, looking carefully for CCTV cameras and other security installations inside the supermarket. Once in a while, one of the terrorists would find a security camera, raise his gun and shoot it down.

Meanwhile, sporadic gunfire continued within and without the precincts of the entire mall especially when the other terrorists were out of sight in the lower floor. It looked like they were searching every nook and cranny of the building. The captives could no longer tell the time nor could they tell whether anyone was making any effort to rescue them. The only signs of life outside the mall were the frequent sirens from ambulances and police cars and the whine of helicopters. Once in a while, the terrorists would discover somebody hiding somewhere within the mall and they would quickly apprehend them, then deal with them depending on whether the captive was male or female. At one point, an air vent high up in the roof of the mall opened and somebody looked out. Whoever it was must have thought the ordeal was over because the premises had gone quiet somewhat. One of the terrorists was however attracted by the movement and without thinking twice, he shot at the figure up there. The lifeless body of a nine or ten year old girl fell from the ceiling and clattered somewhere within the supermarket. Apart from the sharp breaths that were drawn, nobody in the frightened crowd uttered a sound. Amy still hoped that they'd somehow ride out the storm.

The good terrorist finally came up with another one and summoned his colleague who was watching over the hostages. A hurried conference was held at the end of the corridor. The three appeared to come to some decision and leaving the other two terrorists there, the good one went over to the group of hostages and addressed them. What they had agreed remained to be seen.

'We want to separate the wheat from the chaff,' he said. 'If you are Muslim, we will let you go but non-Muslims will be retained here until we decide what to do with them.'

He went over to his colleagues again and stood there talking in low tones with them for some time. They talked into their radios and mobile phones for some time then he came back with one of the terrorists.

'Each one of you will come over here and we will ask you a question. If you know the answer, you will stand aside. If you don't, you will join the group back there,' he said looking down at the hostages like Moctezuma II, the Aztec king, pronouncing judgment on war abductees.

The group stirred but there was no indication as to what kind of questions the terrorists had for the hostages. They simply hurdled together and waited. Then the examination began without ado. There were thirty people hurdled there. Six of them were male. Over three quarters of the remainder were women and the rest were teenage girls. The men were the first to go. The girls couldn't tell what was being asked but out of the six men, two were detained while the rest returned to the hurdled group. They were trying to create the illusion of fairness but it was a poor apology of putting lipstick on a pig.

When the turn came for the two girls, it was Amy who went first. By then, the group had been reduced by about a quarter who had been escorted to the landing of the stairs where they stood waiting. Amy walked over to the masked terrorist whose only sign of life was the hard dark eyes that looked at her. He appeared to resent her innocent light-skinned face immediately he saw it.

'What religion do you practice?' the terrorist asked her looking hard at her eyes as if he expected her to tell a lie.

'What?' Amy returned innocently.

'I asked you who you pray to. Stop kidding me!' the harsh voice went a notch higher, his face wearing a "been there done that" look.

'I pray to God,' Amy answered confused. She wondered whether it was possible to pray to anyone else - or anything else for that matter.

'Who is your God? Answer me girl and stop playing with my mind,' the terrorist gave her the rough edge of his tongue.

'I don't know what you mean. I only know God as God,' the young girl returned looking visibly confused.

'Stop playing with me! Recite the Shahada quickly!' the terrorist said working himself up into a fine anger and pointing at Amy with the ugly muzzle of his rifle. She did not even hear the word properly.

'Recite the what?' she asked desperately.

'You don't know!' It wasn't a question. 'C'mon, stand up and join the other infidels!' It was clear that the terrorist thought he was being given the run-around.

Amy stood up shaken and walked quickly back to the group she had just left. Reasoning with the terrorist was like hitting one's head against a brick wall. The small of her back felt tight as the muzzle of the gun followed her all the way back until she was seated. She felt sure she was between a rock and a hard place. It was Raj's turn to face the music next and the experience of her friend left her sweating. She hobbled up to where the terrorist waited and stood there her eyes focused somewhere between her feet.

'What religion do you practice?' the terrorist who had a finger in every pie said harshly.

He seemed to have decided in advance that she subscribed to some other religion other than the one he personally approved of.

'I'm a Muslim,' she said without raising her eyes to look at him.

'You lie! You don't look Muslim! Who was the mother of the Prophet?' the terrorist asked her unceremoniously, riding roughshod over the innocent girl. Raj hesitated a second before she replied.

'Aminah bint Wahb,' she said looking straight at him.

The terrorist seemed taken back. He appeared to think he was being taken for a ride; he looked at her as if she had just been told what to say by someone else. The fact that this girl could be Muslim was, to him, was a bitter pill to swallow.

'Recite the Shahada,' the terrorist commanded switching to Arabic.

The girl hesitated for another split second.

'There is no god but God, Muhammad is the messenger of God,' the girl said quickly in Arabic.

It was clear she had no clue what this was about.

'Allah have mercy on you,' the terrorist said.

His voice had softened and his hand gesture as he guided Raj away from the rest of the group seemed a lot calmer than before. All the same, Raj cringed as from the touch of a corpse. It felt as if religion was a drug and the lines uttered by Raj had calmed the terrorist like a shot of morphine. She was guided to the landing of the stairs where she joined another smaller group there. It was then that it occurred to her what the terrorists were doing. They were trying to differentiate the Muslims from the non-Muslims and to separate them. The best way to do that would only be to ask everyone who was the Prophet's mother and if somebody hazarded a guess, they were sure he or she could not recite the Shahada therefore the person could not possibly be Muslim. She realized that her friend had little chance of getting out of there alive. Amy was a Catholic Christian. She knew nothing about Islam and could neither tell who the mother of the prophet was nor could she recite a single word of the Shahada. It occurred to her too that if her parents had been detained, her mother and her father had probably been separated from each other in the same way. Her mother was a devout Hindu with antecedents from southern India while her father had kept the Muslim faith which his Pakistani grandfather had immigrated to Kenya with a little over a century ago. It was peculiar how the terrorists could pretend to be good to some people and use that goodness to justify violence on other people – like robbing Peter to pay Paul, Raj thought.

Raj looked over at Amy who sat among the group she had just left. Amy wasn't looking at her but even from that far, she could clearly read the fear on her friend's face. She keenly felt responsible for anything that was likely to happen to her. She had begged Amy to accompany her to Westlands. For the first time in her life, she felt odd to be a Muslim. She felt like she was in league with the terrorists in persecuting everyone else at the Mall. Her religion hung over her heavily like a deep heat blanket and for the first time, she resented it. She remembered how she had often defended her religion in school and especially in 2W being one of the only three Muslims. She had felt relegated when the other students went to worship on Sunday and especially because she and the other thirty or so Muslims in school had to look for something to do for they were not allowed in the dormitories when the Christians went to church, to Shah Hall or to the various other rooms that were used for such services. Nothing like that happened on Friday when she went to pray; learning went on as usual. And even that Friday visit to the mosque only happened when there was a special Muslim occasion such as Ramadan. For the first time since she had joined St. Mary's, the irony of Shah Hall also struck her like a sledge hammer. The hall had been donated by an Ismaili Muslim businessman from Syria named Shah. He visited the school often and never questioned the fact that the hall was used mainly for Christian services. He had even attended one or two services himself! It was true that religion was in one's heart, Raj thought. She had felt too that the Muslims ought to be given Friday off because the Christians had Sunday off. But she had noted that there were other religious groups too who were neither Muslim nor Christian but none of whom felt this segregation as keenly as the Muslims did. It occurred to her too that even at home, her mother had never been so keen about her religion the way she and her father were. That now seemed odd.

The terrorists had now separated the wheat from the chaff. Out of the group of about thirty people, nine had been taken aside and she was among them. There was another teenage girl beside her, four men and three women. The only other two men had been kept apart while the rest of the group hurdled where she had been. The two men looked like quarantined camels which had been separated from the general herd to prevent their infecting it with Mers Camel flu.

'It is time to teach everyone a lesson. We can't let you rock the boat any longer,' the harsh terrorist who obviously had a heart of stone said walking over to the two men.

Before anyone could tell what was happening, he plucked one man by the collar and led him to the edge of the corridor where safety metal railings overlooked the lower floor. Without blinking, he shot him twice through the head and threw him over the railing onto the lower floor. His body clattered downstairs with the noise of scattering hardware. The women screamed but fell silent forthwith when the terrorist turned the smoking muzzle of his gun on them and shouted for silence.

The good terrorist looked at him and shouted something in Arabic. He took the other man by the collar and led him back to the group of condemned hostages where he dumped him brusquely, then went over to the nine Muslims who were waiting at the landing.

'You will be escorted out of the here but anyone who tries to run or help the ones outside will be shot,' he said harshly.

Raj was at a crossroads. There was no way she was going anywhere. She could not leave Amy there while it was she who had led her here yet she felt that any attempt to defy the terrorist could easily lead to her own death and probably that of others. As she was struggling with the turbulence in her soul, the good terrorist came over and said something to the other terrorist in a language she could not understand. He walked over to the condemned group and stood there training his gun on them.

'C'mon,' the good terrorist said. 'We will walk slowly to the entrance and you will make your exit. We have no obligations towards you and I must warn you any sign of defiance will lead to your being shot on the spot.' He did not mince words. 'C'mon, let's go!' he ordered.

Many of the people in the group had little choice but to turn and head down the stairs. Raj made her decision then. She had to roll with the punches.

'I can't go anywhere,' she boldly told the terrorist.

She had never stood up to a terrorist but she appeared ready to get her feet wet.

'What did you say?' the terrorist demanded.

'I said I cannot leave my friend here. I brought her here. I have looked after her for close to one year and I cannot stop here. I'll be left here to share whatever fate will befall her.' Raj often bent over backwards for other people.

'Look here woman,' the terrorist said in a mixture of Arabic and Swahili, 'I am doing you a great favour. You have no choice but to leave or you will compel me to shoot you!'

He raised his rifle and pointed it at her. Raj felt wrong to be addressed as woman. The other people in the group shielded her with their bodies as they tried to appeal to her common sense.

'These people will be saved somehow,' somebody whispered eagerly to her. 'If you make these people any angrier, you'll jeopardize everybody's life including your own.'

'The less people they have to use as a bargaining chip the better for everyone,' a woman who sounded like she had got her fingers burnt before whispered to her. 'Please come with us.'

'Once outside we will make every effort to ensure your friend is saved,' another man said. 'But the best thing to do for now, common sense demands that we leave and try to help the others as much as we can from the outside.'

'You will be of little help to your friend if you are killed,' someone whispered, 'And that may even put her in worse danger.'

'Sorry,' Raj said, 'But my mind is made. I brought that girl here and I'm solely responsible for her safety. I cannot leave.' She steadily pushed through the human wall that was shielding her.

'You'll have to shoot me, I'm sorry,' she told the now visibly agitated terrorist. 'I cannot leave my friend here.'

She calmly walked past the angry man, her back contracting coldly as she waited for the burst of gunfire to rip through her and end her life. The short walk to the other group seemed endless but she made it and rejoined the group she had left a few moments earlier. There was a tense moment as everyone waited to see what the evidently angry terrorists would do. The harsh one went quickly over to the two girls and yanked Amy by her hair and dragged her to the railing as Raj who had risen with her held on desperately to her friend.

'You want me to shoot her and save you the trouble? Yes? Yes?' the terrorist asked her angrily and before she knew it he was swinging her friend back and forth by her hair.

Nothing short of someone's head on a silver platter could calm him. Everybody held their breath as they waited for the gun report like they had done less than ten minutes earlier.

'Omar!' the other terrorist shouted.

Somehow, the two terrorists looked chalk and cheese. He said something else rapidly in Arabic or some such language which stayed the hand of his furious colleague. He added something else and his colleague who was frothing at the mouth already let go of the hapless girl's hair. He pushed the two girls back to the group that was seated further away and ordered everyone in the group to empty their pockets. He collected various items - purses, phones and other personal effects, going through the pockets to search anyone he wasn't satisfied with. He took his booty away and went over to the group standing at the landing then with the muzzle of his rifle motioned them down the stairs leaving the other calmer terrorist to guard the hostages.

5: A revelation

Darkness was falling outside by the time the other terrorist returned. His rushing up the stairs had been preceded by a loud gun report from downstairs. He seemed even more worked up than before as he approached his colleague who, on seeing him, approached him and held a brief guttural conversation. The newcomer motioned downstairs angrily. In his absence, his colleague had appeared unable to make up his mind what to do with the rebellious girl. He had led her to the other group and sat her down angrily before going over to lean against the railing to try to compose himself. He hadn't appeared to trust himself enough to approach the group again after that. The group itself sat there wondering at the madness of the short Indian girl who had dared stand up to a crazed terrorist.

Meanwhile, the two girls sat hurdled together at one corner of the group. Amy had reached out to the hand of her friend and held it immediately they had rejoined the other hostages. She wondered at the calm courage of the girl she had called 'mother' for close to one year. She wasn't sure she would have shown half her courage had she been in Raj's shoes. She could not dare thank her aloud but she squeezed her hand gratefully and her friend understood. As they sat there, the terrorists talked silently among themselves, then the good one went over to the railing and looked down at the lower floor. They could not tell what he was looking at down there but soon their questions were answered. Suddenly, at the head of the stairs, a black shock of hair emerged then they saw the red face underneath it. It was one of the Muslim men who had been led downstairs. Then another followed. Then followed one of the three women and one teenage girl with whom they had gone downstairs. They came onto the landing and stood there looking at the two terrorists. The harsh terrorist who had been called Omar went over to them quickly and using the barrel of his gun herded them over to the condemned group where he pushed them roughly into sitting positions. The teenage girl squeezed between Amy and Raj.

'We couldn't leave after what you did,' she said quietly as she addressed Raj. She sounded like she had nearly had kittens.

'What was that gunshot downstairs about?' Raj asked her unobtrusively.

'He shot one woman. It was she who dissuaded us from going out. Her death hardened our resolve.'

'We need to stick together no matter what,' Amy said. 'Our resistance is breaking their determination,' she whispered.

'I think we need to get talking to the tall one – the one in a white shirt. I feel we can appeal to his rationale if we talk,' Raj said.

'None of these people is willing to negotiate,' the new girl said. 'The last vestige of courage went with the woman they have just killed.'

Amy could not help but agree with her. Although she looked afraid, it was clear she had her head screwed on. However she still felt it is haste that makes waste.

'It might not be a good idea,' Amy whispered. 'It might even enrage them further. It does seem like they all have each other's back.'

'But we can't keep quiet,' Raj insisted. 'They seem to be waiting for something and I feel that something will be our undoing when it finally comes.'

Her argument seemed to hold water but everyone else kept quiet feeling caught in the crossfire. The other two terrorists had not returned and it appeared like they were keeping vigil somewhere. They must have known that eventually, somebody would come and try to rescue the hostages. Definitely, although the rescuers certainly had their hands full, some plan or other was already afoot by then. The people who had been released must have told the rescuers outside how the situation was. The white woman had seemed intelligent enough to do just that. It looked like the terrorists knew and were waiting for that to happen. If that was the case, Amy thought, then it could only mean one thing. They were waiting for rescuers so that they could go down with as many people as possible. They had no intention of saving anyone out of the group that was left, not even the Muslims.

'Raj,' Amy whispered, 'the way I read this, it looks like they are waiting for the ripe time for a mass suicide.'

'Why do you think so?' she whispered back.

'It isn't like they are waiting to negotiate with anyone. I can only make out four of them and white shirt looks like their commander. He hasn't left here. He hasn't made any demands on anyone.' Amy returned.

'Might they have done that from somewhere else? Why is it that he has a soft spot for us?' the new girl wondered.

'He can't have made any demands. He has been with us since the situation calmed down somewhat. We would have heard him talk to someone else apart from those he has been talking to in Arabic,' Raj whispered.

'There's something else. No negotiator would be willing to kill people. It puts him at a disadvantage,' Amy said.

'And the more hostages he has the better it would be for him. These are not negotiators. I've told you what they just did downstairs,' the new girl seconded the motion.

Just then, the good terrorist approached them and the girls had to fall silent again.

'I want to warn you again that no rebellion will be tolerated again. Those who have chosen to come back have done so of their own free will. Sit with everyone else and await your fate. May Allah have mercy upon you.'

He went further away to stand near the railing. The other terrorist had gone downstairs. Nobody knew where the other two were. Indeed, nobody could tell whether there were others in other parts of the mall but since they had seen the four at various times during the afternoon's ordeal, the girls assumed that the terrorists had been in a gang of four. It was also clear by now that white shirt was their commander. It was not possible to have a second commander and the girls felt confident that had there been more terrorists, they would have been bound to come for instructions from white shirt at one time or another. The gang seemed well-trained and well-coordinated and they did everything military style.

'You know you should let everyone go,' Raj said loudly out of the blue.

Amy's heart missed a beat while everyone else gaped at her friend because of her audacity. Her bravery was second nature. For some time she had looked like she had a bee in her bonnet. Her boldness made White Shirt's heckles rise. He did not look around as he spoke.

'I don't need opinions from anyone here, is that clear?' There was some silence as everyone listened to their heartbeats.

'You are Muslim like me,' Raj said loudly again, then paused for some reaction from the terrorist but he kept his cool. 'Islam is a peaceful religion and what you are doing is violent,' she ploughed on.

White shirt shifted his position at the railing but did not comment, neither did he turn around. He didn't seem like he'd ever see the error of his ways. Everyone else held their breath.

'The prophet was the most peaceful of all people...that is why we keep quoting 'peace be upon him'...it is sacrilegious to Islam and to the prophet to use the religion to justify violence,' Raj pursued relentlessly.

'Woman, you will keep quiet about violence! What do you know about violence?' White shirt demanded turning aggressively and facing her.

The assembled people gaped at her wondering how she plucked courage to stand up to a terrorist! The mind boggles! Raj wondered again why the terrorist kept thinking of her as a woman. Was it to lessen her innocence, thus justify her condemnation? She kept quiet for half a minute until the terrorist looked away then continued.

'I know that violence gnaws at a man's soul and evil begets evil. That is what the good book teaches. Violence blinds a man so that he can no longer tell the difference between what is right and what is wrong,' the young girl said philosophically.

Those around her gawked at both her calm nature and her insight not
to mention the eloquence with which she spoke. Amy saw her friend in
a new light for the first time.

'You would think different if you had people invade your country and try to root out Islam in the name of fundamentalism. We aren't shying away from violence until all the Kenyans and Americans are out of Somalia. We are prepared to give as good as we get.'

'So your problem is that there are people who have invaded your country? Where does Islam come in? Has it crossed your mind that there are people in Somalia who aren't Muslim? What excuse are they using to export terrorism to other people?' she did not mince words.

Raj, who had the gift of the gab was so persuasive she could sell ice to the Eskimos.

'Woman you are getting on my nerves. And you're too clever for your own good. There are people in this world who have vowed to exterminate Islam and we must face them head on. They say might is right and therefore, the law of the jungle must rule for some time.'

It looked like he was going to great lengths to maintain his calm, but terrorism and irascibility go hand in hand, of course.

'Let's stick to Islam and Somalia for a minute. That's the subject you brought up. Who was aggressive to the other first, the Muslim fundamentalists in Somalia or the innocent Kenyans whose blood you are shedding here?'

'Do not ask me a lot of foolish questions. We have a mission here to send a message to the Kenyan government to get out of Somalia and that is all I care!'

'You bombed buildings in Nairobi and killed Kenyans long before they came to your country, isn't that right?'

'Yes, because that was the only way to get the message to their American friends,' the terrorist said heatedly.

'It appears you aren't sure who you want to fight, the Americans or Kenyans, Christians or infidels. Or are you just a messenger who knows little about what he has been sent to do? You do not seem sure whether it is Americans or Kenyans you have a quarrel with...and it takes two to tango. If you find it necessary to quarrel with the Americans, then you are as bad as they are. You similarly seemed perplexed whether to kill us because we are Kenyans or whether to simply kill those who aren't Muslims.' Raj picked holes at the terrorist's picture perfect logic.

'All I know is that the Americans and their Jew infidel friends will have to learn a lesson. It is our job to even the score and I do not care whether Kenyans die in the process or not!'

'So if you kill us you'll be even Stevens? For how long will you live a lie? There is no American or Jew here. Maybe you just missed them. And infidels are people without religion. I doubt whether there is anyone here who doesn't know God. Before you criticize a man, walk a mile in his shoes!' Raj gave him a piece of her mind.

The terrorist did not say anything though his nature changed little. He simply seemed angry that a Muslim girl was reasoning with him and he couldn't ignore her, neither could he just shoot her. The girl had to have gone out of her mind.

'Both Christianity which you are busy fighting in the name of infidelity and Islam itself are not African,' Raj pursued inexorably. 'They have been sheltered here by Africans the way a guest is shown a room to spend the night. Is it right then for both religions to fight in the house and kill the Africans who have accommodated them?'

'Woman, you know not what you talk about,' the terrorist said looking away as a lost look crept into his eyes. The rest of the group had followed the altercation silently as they looked from one face to the other. 'I didn't expect a child like you to understand anything anyhow.'

He did appear a little baffled that somebody was poking so many holes into his pie-in-the-sky idea of solving the problems of the world.

'A moment ago you called me a woman, didn't you?' Raj paused. 'Until today I was thinking like you,' she continued. 'I'm torn between Hinduism and Islam, Africa my adopted domicile and Asia where my germ is. Who says it is not possible for me to accommodate all these. Who says that man must live by choice?'

'Like I said, we are here to send a message that Kenya must withdraw from Somalia. An eye for an eye and a tooth for a tooth! I don't care what *you* think!'

'Mahatma Gadhi once said that an eye for an eye will leave the whole world blind. And you can't treat all people the same way – it is different strokes for different folks. Why do you teach your children to come conduct similar suicidal missions here for you? Why don't you tell them the truth? Why do you feed on their blood like the proverbial Dheg-Dheer?'

The terrorist seemed to jump at the mention of the monster. He appeared not to expect the young girl to know of any such thing. At some point, it felt like Raj was playing into the hands of the bloodthirsty terrorists. The two went at it hammer and tongs.

'We must learn to stick together, to quote Brenda Fassie. That is the only way to fight out American imperialism and aggression.'

'I'm just a schoolgirl. I would know little about imperialism. I doubt whether you yourself know anything about it. All I know is that every human being, including your own son has a right to determine his own destiny. Many of those who you killed here today know nothing about what cost their lives. You yourself don't appear to understand why you are killing,'

Raj looked the man straight in the eye. She could not tell exactly what he felt because of his covered face but she thought his eyes did change. His silence and the way he looked at her suggested that he was no longer sure of himself as he had been earlier. She had to buy time for all the hostages.

'The Prophet does not condone death of the innocent, neither does the Koran,' Raj fine-tuned her argument. 'If you can't fight the Americans, it is foolish to look for scapegoats among Kenyans. I myself cannot claim to be Kenyan but I am glad for the peace the country gives me. I respect the fact that it has hosted me. I'm very sure I would most probably be dead by now if I had been brought up in my violent

Asian homeland. I'm not sure what you are but I can tell that you know what you are doing here is wrong. And the only human being in this world without a conscience is a sick one. You don't look sick like your colleague who went downstairs. Don't act like it. You have a mind of your own.' Raj could really talk the hind leg off a hog if she put her mind to it.

Had the circumstances been different, the gathered people would have applauded but they still looked at the Indian girl as if she didn't have a stitch on; Raj did nothing by halves. They contented themselves at marveling at the short girl who was wise way beyond her years. They were happy too that she was buying them some time.

'Some of you don't even look Somali or Arab,' Raj continued. 'I'm sure you've been converted recently, then you were promised money to do what you are doing. Why? Because those Muslims who use you this way know it is wrong. And only a Muslim who hasn't read the Koran properly would do what you are doing. Islam is peaceful, the prophet is peaceful. Whose violence guides you?' Raj was quiet for some time. 'How much are they paying you to come here and kill innocent women and children? Or are you after the proverbial seven virgins? Who tells you the virgins will accept murderers?'

'This is not about money woman...and you need to mind your own business now,' the terrorist rasped.

He did not look at anyone in the group. His eyes deliberately avoided those of Raj. Amy sat there looking at the Indian girl who had taken her under her wing; it made her feel like a fifth wheel.

'You are sure if we check your bank account we won't see any evidence of a recent big activity? Why don't you accept that this all has to do with money and politics – that you are doing somebody's dirty work? And why don't they get fifty and sixty year olds to carry out such missions?'

The terrorist was quiet. It was clear that although he was not anywhere near to considering his actions than he had been at the beginning, his thinking had gone down several miles in a way that it hadn't done in the recent past.

'Why do those who send you look for men on the make - young men in need of money to make them do this? Why do you settle the score on someone's behalf? They convince you to give up your life so that the money you are paid to kill can help your families? Whoever heard of blood money benefiting anyone? Why don't they ever agree to go on suicide missions themselves? I'm not very old but I know that life for every human being is their own. And it is sacred and precious. You have as much right to live as any of those who sent you – or those you think your money will go to for that matter.'

'I said this has nothing to do with money!' the terrorist said angrily fighting shy of admitting he was outwitted. Raj's pester power appeared to have softened him a little.

Raj had to pause for some time for the terrorist was looking tensed up as if he regretted some of the things he had done recently. He however didn't look any less ready to die.

'Ever watched a movie called *Little Manhattan*?'

'Western movies are for infidels!'

'Maybe that is why you don't know. There's a little boy there called Ray who is a lot cleverer than you are.' Raj paused. 'He says that you come into this life alone...and you leave it the same way.' She gave him time to absorb that. 'Life is sweet and I'm not ready to give up mine for anyone.' Raj said philosophically after some time. 'That is probably why those who sent you to kill us want to hang onto their own,' she paused. 'I don't agree with America any more than you do. I disagree strongly with what many Americans do. Nobody has the right to overlord another in this world; everyone has as much right to live in it as everyone else. But I don't think coming here to kill innocent African children and calling them infidels is advancing your cause any further than it was when the prophet died. May peace be upon him! In any case, if anyone asked me, we Muslims should unite with these Africans to stop westerners from exploiting them and us. That's the way to solve the problem. You can't deal with an aggressive neighbour by turning your frustrations against a weaker one, can you?' Raj hammered the point home. The situation had reached fever pitch.

'Now you will have to keep your mouth shut!' the terrorist said, cheesed off and turning to the teenage girl with the pointed gun. His bark sent a shiver down the spines of all assembled there. 'And to set the record straight, I do not care whether you are a girl or a woman. An infidel is an infidel! Any more nonsense from any of you here and you'll all be dead meat.'

Footsteps were heard coming up the stairs and presently, two other terrorists appeared at the head of the stairs. They signaled to the one who had been guarding the group and he walked over to them. They held a brief conversation in what sounded like Arabic, then white shirt went down stairs. He came back shortly and said something to the other terrorists who went downstairs leaving him there to guard the hostages. He pulled out his radio and talked at length into it. Then he began pacing up and down the length of the railing. After a short while, one of the terrorists came back. He carried loaves of bread, bottles of water and cans of soda. He dumped them unceremoniously on the floor before the group of hostages.

'Help yourselves,' white shirt said. 'It's likely to be a long night.'

You could see that he considered this small sacrifice chicken feed out of which he could reap a lot more. He walked away and went to stand near the railing, his eyes trained on the floor below. The ensuing silence was so deep you could have heard a pin drop. The hostages didn't need to understand rocket science to know that theirs was a tar baby situation.

6: Breaking the Ranks

'I think we have to act quickly if we are to live,' the Muslim girl who had come with the other defiant group from downstairs told the two school girls.

'Why?' Raj who was down in the dumps whispered.

'I understand Arabic,' she continued. 'The one in a white shirt has been talking to someone on the radio. I heard him saying time is not yet ripe.'

'What does he mean by that?' it was Amy's turn to wonder.

'I'm not sure,' the girl said. 'But it is all clear that they are waiting for something big. Acting now may give us a good head start.'

'Then you've got to listen very carefully and try to decide what it is they intend to do with us. That is the only way we can probably convince everyone else that we need to do something,' Raj said.

Amy looked up at her friend thinking how she had told the terrorist a thing or two. She was used to her friend hiding a light under a bushel but this new Raj was completely baffling.

'You were really brave there,' she said, 'You think we can make it out of here as a group?'

'We'll need to test the waters...'

'And this guy here,' the Muslim girl interrupted quietly as she indicated one of the men with whom they had returned upstairs with her pulled lips. 'I think he is one of them.'

'What do you mean?' Raj said horrified.

'He's been acting funny – preaching water and drinking wine. There is something about him which I can't put my finger on. Downstairs he tried to convince us to leave. He said that no Muslim should die with infidels. I was surprised to see him come back with us.'

'Then we need to keep our lips sealed where he is concerned,' Amy who was as close as an oyster said.

'You are right,' Raj concurred. 'We need to keep our discussions on the PQ - in strict confidence I mean.'

It occurred to Amy that she could not tell whether the Muslim girl was on their side or not. Like the other Muslims, she had an air of separated composure about her and she could not really tell whether or not she had a hidden agenda. There was little the girls could do but take the risk and give her the benefit of doubt. Meanwhile, everyone waited. The women reluctantly reached for the bread and soda and tried to taste them, then passed them to those around them. People reluctantly sipped at the soda and water but nobody ate anything. After some time, the man who the Muslim girl had talked about took the bread and continued to munch with little regard to those around him, his head clearly in the clouds. He took to the bread like a duck to water. Many of the other people did not even notice him. A real dog in the manger, the man would benefit nothing by helping the terrorists, Amy thought. When he was through with his bread, the man raised his hand and when the terrorist who was guarding them noticed him, he asked for permission to visit the toilet. He spoke in Swahili with a coastal accent and the others were surprised to see that the terrorist understood him. Before that, it had only appeared like the terrorists only understood Arabic or English - and some other language they used among themselves which to Amy sounded like Somali. The terrorist nodded the man to the end of the long corridor where a door whose frame was tagged 'washrooms' stood open.

The man rose and shuffled his feet down the corridor. The terrorist did not appear unduly concerned about the man's trip to the toilet nor whether it was possible he might find a way to escape. The man took some time before he returned. None of the three girls could tell whether or not it had been a simple trip to attend to a call of nature. He sat back and kept an impassive face.

At dusk, one of the terrorists approached a back room downstairs whose door was open. It appeared like the room the workers at the supermarket used to prepare items for sale before they went to pack them onto the shelves. It was littered with empty boxes and polythene wrappers, scales, weighing machines and stacks of packing bags. The terrorist went and stood just inside the well-lit room and looked around. He cleared some space in the middle of the room then disappeared somewhere within. He spent some time rummaging about, then came out later looking frustrated. He went into the lower floor of the supermarket and looked around, seemed to decide something, then climbed to the first floor and disappeared among the shelves far to the right. Presently, he returned with a Persian rug about a metre and a half in length by a metre in width. He went downstairs with it, then got into the back room in which he had been rummaging a few minutes before. He spread out the rug on the floor, then shouted at one of his colleagues who was somewhere beyond the girls' line of vision. He went over to him and stood guard just outside the door. The other terrorist knelt down on the rug and proceeded to pray. He rose up and held his hands up in supplication, then knelt and touched his forehead on the rug at intervals.

Raj looked down at the praying form and clicked her tongue. Who did he hope to appeal to after what he had done? Did he think that God was that narrow minded to be bribed so shortly after life He had given had so cruelly been taken away without his permission? Raj wondered at the irony of the actions of the terrorists. How could anyone prostrate himself to appeal to God after shedding so much blood? If he died, like she felt very sure he would, did he expect God to receive him with blood of the innocent still tainting his hands? Or was he already atoning for what he had done, and what he was probably about to do? It was all very confusing. When the first terrorist was through, he went to stand guard while his colleague took his turn on the Persian rug, *stolen Persian rug*, it occurred to Raj. What hypocrisy clouded this world!

When they were through, the two terrorists went their way leaving the door to the back room open. The one who was guarding them did not seem keen on prayer. It occurred to Raj that his conscience had thawed somewhat though there was no indication that the hostages were in any less danger. He continued talking animatedly on his radio and on the various phones he carried on his person. Now and then, he appeared to consort a broad piece of paper which he carried in the pocket of his jacket, then give instructions as he looked down at it.

'You know what?' the Muslim girl beside the two girls said. 'I think we are in a lot of danger.'

'Why?' The other two girls chorused. 'What's wrong?' Amy added.

'From what that guy is saying on the radio, it appears they are wiring up this building with explosives. I think he let the cat out of the bag by speaking so near to us.'

'Oh my God,' a woman who had heard her said as she caught her breath sharply.

'How do you know?' Raj asked the girl.

'He seems to be directing the other terrorists to different parts of the building. I would even say there must be more than the four who've been in and out of this supermarket,' she said.

'Where the hell does that leave us?' Amy wondered aloud.

'And there's more,' the girl continued. 'It appears there is someone he keeps telling "Time is not ripe! Time is not ripe!" I'm not sure whether he is arguing with his colleagues or whether he is trying to stay them until something he is waiting for happens but he looks set to wait until his own sweet time.'

'So what do we do? Do we sit here and wait to die like penned sheep or do we risk and run for our lives?' a woman asked behind them.

'Come on, let your hair down. I would still say we wait and shop around for ideas; running for it like headless chicken may do more harm than good. Whatever they are waiting for doesn't appear about to happen. I think we should buy more time and try to talk to him when he comes nearer,' Amy said.

'I'm not waiting for that to happen. I'll think on my feet and take my chances; nothing ventured, nothing gained,' a man to Raj's left said.

Before anyone could react, the man who had chickened out rose and ran towards the railing to the left, away from the terrorist who was

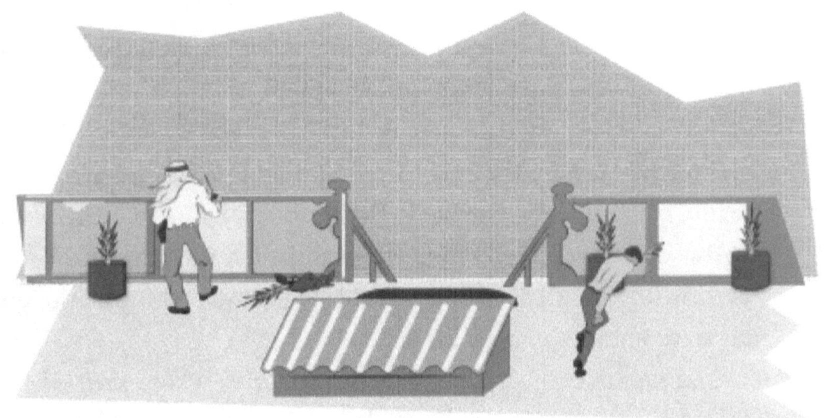

Before anyone could react, the man who had chickened out rose and ran towards the railing to the left...

keeping guard. It was clear he had decided to chance his arm. The terrorist had a rude awakening. He was so much taken by surprise that he wheeled around suddenly, his gun aimed at the group before he realized there was somebody running away towards the other side of the long corridor. He said something sharply in Arabic as the running man hoisted himself over the railing and poised himself to jump onto the floor below. There was brief dramatic delay like the sudden stop of the action in a movie as a hero and the villain face up, then the man jumped high into the air. The rifles suddenly opened up and they seemed to hold the body of the man briefly in midair as bullets ripped through him, then he was gone and the cowering group could no longer see him. A moment later, there was a loud crash as his body landed on something downstairs cracking it open with the combined sound of sharp glass and dry wood. Then there was silence. Nobody had time to react and by the time they recovered, it was too late to even scream. They sat there petrified. The terrorists had also been taken by surprise. There was a brief moment of disbelief, then the terrorist who was guarding the little group reacted. He came rushing at the group and seized another man by his hair.

'You want action huh? Huh?' the terrorist, whose avowed intent was to discipline everyone, demanded of no one in particular. 'You will get some action,' he declared ruthlessly.

He led his victim to the railing where the man who had died in a hail of bullets had jumped barely a minute before. He shot his victim twice in the chest before their very eyes and threw him over the railing onto the lower floor.

'Sit tight!' the terrorist who had gone bananas declared at the general gathering. 'We all go together, you hear?' he asked angrily then walked quickly away to stand near the railing training his gun at the lower floor.

The horrified group cringed deeper into themselves, their hearts in their mouths. The three girls held more tightly to one another as other people moaned softly.

'We are done, we are done for!' a woman cried silently. 'Lord do not forget us! Remember us the way you remembered your disciples.'

The group sat there unthinking for some time. Everyone could see that any plans of getting away had gone pear shaped. The terrorist guarding them was also quiet and the only sound heard apart from the low music coming from somewhere above them was the static from his radio. He seemed as tensed up as his captives and appeared particularly frustrated that he was unable to tell where the music eating at his nerves was coming from. Several times, two of the terrorists had looked up there as if trying to identify where the speakers were hidden. They had shot up there severally and only once had one of them been able to mute a speaker somewhere to their left. The others appeared hidden where they couldn't see them. The group could still hear Foreigner somewhere up there singing *Waiting for a Girl Like You*. It emphasized the irony of their circumstances making their loneliness even worse.

'God we can't simply be sitting ducks. The chips are down and there's a lot at stake,' Amy pleaded to no one in particular. 'These terrorists are deliberately dragging their feet about our fate.'

'What can we do? You've just seen what awaits you if you try anything,' the Muslim girl said.

It was all she could do to keep from trembling. She felt like she had a chip on her shoulder because she was Muslim.

'Our best bet is getting a grip on ourselves and thinking straight,' Raj said. 'It is too early to accept defeat. We are still strong. We must preserve both our energies and our sane minds for whatever is to come.'

'We are chasing rainbows here – we aren't going anywhere. We are doomed!' someone moaned. 'God has forgotten us.'

Although they couldn't tell what time it was, it was clear that darkness had already settled on the troubled city for the light inside the supermarket had grown dimmer. Many of the electric lights in there had been shot down and the few lighting it from very high up they were shedding little hooded light. The fact that it had grown darker proved that sunlight had already gone. A phone started vibrating somewhere near Amy scaring her stiff. She realized it was with the Muslim man who had been granted permission to visit the toilet. Everyone wondered how he had been able to hide it when they had been searched although no one commented. It had no ring tone and therefore the terrorist who was guarding them did not notice. The man removed it from his pocket quickly and silenced it. When the terrorist came near them again, one of the women spoke.

'Can you at least let us go and relieve ourselves?'

The terrorist considered that. At this stage in the game, he did not want to jeopardize what he had already gained. He walked slowly to the end of the corridor, opened the door to the washrooms using the barrel of his gun and looked inside. He seemed satisfied before he turned and came back leaving the door open. He looked round at the ragged group of hostages before he spoke.

'One at a time,' he said getting a change of heart and looking around. 'You!' he said pointing at the Muslim man who had a phone. 'You guard them and make sure only one leaves at a time. And the door remains open.'

The woman who had asked about the toilets was the first to go. Nobody looked in the direction she went. She spent a minute in there then came back. A few more people went to the toilet before Amy nudged her friend.

'Go on,' she told Raj looking kindly at the round light-skinned face with hints of red pimples on the cheeks and the forehead.

'No, you go,' Raj said good-naturedly. 'A mother should be able to hold longer than a daughter.' There was little mirth in her voice.

Amy rose, put her best foot forward and went self-consciously down the long corridor. Although she had bells on, she avoided looking over the railing at the remains of the man who had jumped downstairs or the one shot immediately afterwards. At the end of the corridor, she realized there was some recess to the right through which she could see a door marked 'Ladies'. Apparently, the gents must have been on the other side. Opposite the recess, she saw a door marked 'Emergency Exit'. It had been made to open inwards but had been barred by long metal bars which were secured in the centre by a big shiny silver padlock. This would be their way out if things came to that, she thought. Hanging in front of the door was a fire extinguisher whose red shoulder was covered in dust. It was clear it had rarely been used, if at all. She went into the toilet. The toilet door opened onto a space with three open doors. The floor was tiled with beautiful flowery tiles and the sit-on toilet bowls rose to near her knee. There were no water closets but a shiny silver push button with a red dot in the middle which was marked 'push' released a torrent of water when she pushed. The toilet flushed with a subdued gurgling noise. She noted all these things in the half minute it took her to go into the toilet and come out. She walked back to the sitting hostages feeling between the devil and the deep blue sea and nodded to her friend.

'Your turn,' she said. Raj rose and headed for the toilets.

The Muslim man who had been assigned to watch over them kept watch without appearing to. He looked at everyone who rose from the corner of his eye, escorted them down the corridor with an eagle eye and did the same as they came back. Meanwhile, the terrorist who was guarding them looked on from a distance away where he leaned on the railing appearing to be as disinterested in what the little group was doing as possible. He however kept his gun trained on them and the barrel imperceptibly pointed down the corridor when anyone went down to the toilet. A little relieved after their ablutions, the group sat there trying to think each in his or her own way. They remembered friends and relatives at home and wished they had been a little keener to enjoy their company. The mothers missed the ordinary disturbing cries of their babies and the many nagging wants of their children which they had often taken for granted. Their runaway thoughts would rudely be brought back to the present every now and then when a burst of rifle fire rang through the hollow silence of the building or came as a distant report from somewhere outside the building.

7: A Long Wait in the Night

Although they had sank their teeth into the new activities, many of the girls parked at the Parklands Police station found it near impossible to hold any longer when it appeared that the lockdown at the Westgate mall would take a lot longer than had been anticipated. They turned to Mr. Maranga.

'Sir, I think some of us ought to go up there and ascertain exactly what is going on,' Mak broached the subject to their teacher. 'We've got to keep a finger on the pulse of the new developments there.'

The girls near her agreed with her.

'It feels evil to sit here and listen to gunshots ringing through the air without in any way trying to find out exactly what is happening to our colleagues. We ought to have done so ages ago,' Julie observed.

'No girls. That ship has sailed. Let bygones be bygones and focus on the future,' Teacher Lillian said. 'We have agreed to your helping here but that is it. We cannot allow anyone of you near that dangerous place.'

'Yes,' Mr. Maranga quipped. 'You need to bite the bullet on this one. Besides, you are only likely to bring knives to a gunfight and I'm not willing to put any of you girls in any more danger than you are already in.'

'Sir,' Mak insisted as was characteristic of her, 'We aren't in any danger. And even if we were, what can be said of those two girls inside that besieged building?'

'That, as sensible as it is Chima, cannot be used to let you girls out of here. Ms. Konga emphasized clearly that what you people are doing is noble but Mr. Maranga and I are wholly responsible for you. Do not try to stretch already taut nerves,' Teacher Lillian appealed.

She seemed to know very well that the girls could talk their way into Mr. Maranga's soft side and she felt it her duty to prevent this so as to keep the girls as far from danger as it was possible, their good hearts and intentions notwithstanding.

'But sir,' Julie countered looking at Mr. Maranga whose resolve looked already strained, 'isn't it ironical that we are here sitting on some of our skills in First Aid while many bleeding people rescued out of that building, probably even Amy and Raj themselves sit there and cry for help? We need to do unto others as we would have them do unto us.' It was turning out to be a battle of wills between the girls and their teachers.

'Besides,' Jane Rose said, 'We do very well in making food and coffee but we are giving it for distribution to the very people who're supposed to be holding guns there fighting those nutties.'

Teacher Lillian opened her mouth to speak then thought better of it. She let Mr. Maranga who had hemmed and hawed for some time defend himself.

'Alright, alright...Aaalright!' Mr. Maranga said vexed and nearly angry but deciding he could bend the rules a little. 'I also feel the need to go out there and help but we cannot put ourselves in danger also. Do you realize we will be giving the police there extra work of having to think of those trapped and us too?'

'We can watch from a distance...and be a little bit more useful from there. If this is a rescue operation, then we need to go the whole hog. We can't let the chance slip through our fingers,' Nasibo said.

All this time, few people had turned away from the tasks that had been assigned them. They talked to the teachers and to one another as their hands worked dexterously at some task or other. There was a long silence as the teachers looked at one another. Mr. Maranga recovered first and pulled Teacher Lillian a little away from the girls.

'There's a lot of sense in what the girls are saying,' it was Teacher Lillian who spoke first. 'But I didn't want to show them so openly that I feel with them.'

'I do agree,' Mr. Maranga said, 'But situations such as this could turn out tricky. Anything can happen when our girls are sitting there believing they are good Samaritans.'

'What do you suppose we should do? I also see that it is quite stressing for the girls to sit less than a kilometer away and not be able to tell what is happening to their colleagues.'

'I do concur but I still have my reservations. Having the girls sleep out of school and cook in a police station is bad enough.'

'Desperate times call for desperate measures,' Teacher Lillian said. 'Besides, this is a national issue. I suppose we could let a few of them accompany the police in the Land Cruiser the next time it visits the scene. Those ones can bring back news and ease the tension a little.'

'I'll seek the opinion of the deputy OCS. After all, it is her vehicle and the bulk of it is *her* operation and it looks like she is having her orders carried out to the letter,' Mr. Maranga said finally.

The girls held their breaths as he went to consult with the deputy OCS. When he came back, he had good news for them; it was a done deal and four girls could accompany the police officers at a time. They would help in the distribution of necessities and keep the police officers free to deal with what they knew best; crime. The girls were relieved for they had got to first base although their teachers still warned that they had to stay clear of the dangerous mall. Mr. Maranga added that one of the teachers had to accompany the girls on any such trip.

Naturally, Julie, Mak, Jennifer and Nasibo were the first girls. They got into the police vehicle at some minutes before eight. They were lucky to accompany the deputy OCS herself. She sat in the front cabin and as such, the girls were treated to VIP handling. In the police vehicle was packed food, water, jugs of black coffee and blankets. When they got near the mall, they realized that it had been cordoned off and the police would not allow anyone beyond the hundred metre perimeter from the mall. Even from as far as two hundred metres, people crouched as if in very real danger of being shot. The vicinity was enveloped in fear and foreboding. Their vehicle approached the mall from behind and they had a good view down the long paved street leading to the rear of the mall. Although it was long after dark, people still milled around like swarming termites after a shower, many of them relatives who knew one of their own had been trapped inside the building. The vicinity was awash with the red and blue light of police cars waiting to whisk the rescued to safety and Ambulances waiting for the injured. People milled

 JORGES P. LOPEZ

around in the orange and yellow safety jackets that identified them as rescuers and allowed them to go near the mall every time a victim was pulled out of the building. A little away from the girls, journalists from across the world stood waiting, some with their cameras on tripods. Periodically, they would rise quickly like bees disturbed from a hive and follow some important personality or police officer as they tried to hog details of what was going on to give their media stations an edge over the breaking news.

When the deputy OCS alighted from the vehicle, her uniform drew attention and the journalists rushed at her to get some news.

'Madam what comment do you have on the progress of your officers so far?' one asked.

'Do you think the situation is likely to be diffused before daybreak?' another demanded.

'Can you confirm whether or not there are still hostages in that building,' still another said.

'I'll be on the level here...I'm here for news like all of you,' Amina said curtly as she edged away and approached a number of police officers crouching a little way ahead. They rose as they saw her approach.

The girls watched the light amber building a little way away from them. Though the mall itself did look a little subdued, the serenity of the vicinity belied the seriousness and volatility of what was going on inside it. From where the girls stood, the paved street that led down to the mall looked like any other Nairobi street after sunset. Midway between where the girls were and the point where the street met the mall, there was a small bridge over a tunnel. Though the tunnel had a little water, it looked purposely meant to carry rain water away from the mall and the buildings adjacent to it when it rained so as to prevent flooding. Despite the fact that they could not see exactly where the tunnel came from, it did look like it came from under the mall itself.

Where the vehicle came to rest, there were police officers lounging and waiting to relieve their colleagues who were in the mall. There were also relatives of the missing as well as well-wishers. Many of them lazed about or sat in a small tent that had been erected at the very end of the street. The girls set about serving them with coffee in disposable plastic cups and small brown buns for those with the appetite. They gave blankets to the people inside the tent especially those who had small children. The mothers were especially glad for many had to hold their children in their arms. Now they could at least put the sleeping children on blankets on the floor of the tent. Intermittently, a group of rescuers would hurry up the road carrying an injured victim or an unharmed person who had been rescued from the mall. The people under the tent rushed to ascertain whether it was one of their own, then the victim would be whisked away in an ambulance if badly injured. Those suffering from trauma were handled in another tent down the road. When the girls had served as many people as they could, they went about collecting trash as they had been advised by Amina. They loaded it into trash bags and put it in the police vehicle to be disposed away. Mak and Julie approached a police officer for news.

'Hi, you know there are two of our colleagues in that building?' Mak asked a female police officer.

'Oh? I'm sorry. What happened, I mean how did they find themselves there?' The police officer asked as she looked at their light blue uniform.

'It is a long story. Let's just say they went there to visit somebody.'

'Don't you worry. Our officers are doing the best they can,' the police officer said trying to keep a stiff upper lip.

'How long do you think this is likely to take?' Julie asked.

'There's no way of telling. We have been using the regular police and the AP but I hear there are plans to bring in the military.'

'Really?' Julie brightened up. 'How soon?'

'Again, there is no telling with these things. We are keeping our options open. By all looks and intents, they should probably be here by midnight, dawn at the latest.'

'That's encouraging. I can't bear to think what those girls are going through,' Mak said.

'Glad to see you are still positive,' the police officer said. 'There are many who think that no one is alive apart from the terrorists. Of course that is mere pessimism.'

They were quiet for a while.

'There have been a number of rescues in the last one hour and some of our colleagues say they can still talk to people trapped there,' the police officer clarified.

'All we can do is hope for the best,' Julie said.

'And pray o,' Mak said as she crossed herself.

In its next trip to the police station, the police vehicle took away only two of the girls; Mak and Julie refused to budge and although Mr. Maranga threatened them with fire and brimstone at first, he finally allowed them to stay; he understood that the two were some of the closest friends of the two girls trapped in the mall. In less than half an hour, the vehicle returned with three other girls, Jenny, Jane Rose and Rehema – and Mr. and Mrs. Manji. They said they could not bear to be any further away until it was clear what had happened to their child and her friend. They didn't mind sitting in the open for they had been living in Parklands for donkey's years. Mr. Manji who had become sort of acquainted with Mr. Maranga asked him to clarify how his daughter had become a mother at school. There was humour as Mr. Maranga tried to explain, then Teacher Lillian. Finally, it was Mak who appeared to make sense to the two parents. They nodded and thanked her. She thanked them instead and tried to explain the close relationship between the two St. Maryan girls who had been caught up in the hostage situation.

'Each of us has been a mother to a form one. We are still meant to be but many of us only last the one or two months it takes the Form Ones to acclimatize,' she let off steam as she looked at Mrs. Manji who appeared to have cried her eyes out.

'Accra what?' asked Mrs. Manji who appeared to find the concept rather interesting.

Mak marveled at the concern on the old lady's face. It was true, she mused, what the Irish say; a son is a son till he takes him a wife; a daughter is a daughter all her life.

'Acclimatize. It means getting used to how things happen in a new area,' Mak said.

One could see she was finding it difficult to avoid punctuating her speech with the usual 'o'.

'For a moment there I had thought our daughter was turning immoral,' Mr. Manji said gravely. He had a way of emphasizing his 'th' which made him quite interesting to listen to.

'Your daughter and Amy have struck a relationship that is quite intriguing to us,' Julie said 'She has indeed made many of us feel guilty for shirking our duty.' Looking at her, she marveled at how much Raj was a chip off the old block.

'Makes sense,' Mrs. Manji said. 'She is an only daughter. She had close friends in primary school but none of them went to a boarding school. Most joined Parklands and Aga Khan.'

'Where did she go to school?' Julie asked making conversation.

'Oh, just here at Montessori Basic,' she said waving a hand. 'It is less than a kilometer away,' she said joining the last two words into one and changing the initial 'a' of the last word into an 'e'.

The two girls could see that the old lady had nearly gone to pieces with stress.

'Hey girls,' Mr. Maranga said interrupting them. 'I am sorry but we will have to leave.'

'But why sir?' Julie asked as the girls were taken aback.

'Instructions from school. Somebody gave Ms. Konga news of where we are. I'm not exactly licking anyone's boots but she has ordered that we pack and go right back to school.' He did not mince his words.

'But sir, even if we have to leave without knowledge of our colleagues, can we dare leave this couple here this way?' Julie asked avoiding her teacher's eye.

'Young woman, it is my job on the line. You and I know I wouldn't do this if I didn't feel pushed to the wall,' he said avoiding the eyes of the two girls too. 'You both know that Ms. Konga runs St. Mary's with a heavy hand.'

The girls sat there for some time, then Julie rose to her feet. Mr. Maranga stood there waiting. Mr. and Mrs. Manji were lost for words as they contemplated the long night ahead. The two girls were being taken away just when they had thought they had found company. Mak remained where she was. It looked like their rescue plan was headed for the doldrums.

'Miss Chimaka?' Mr. Maranga asked looking down at the dark Nigerian girl.

'Yes sir,' Mak said.

'C'mon. You know very well I can't fight city hall.'

'I'm afraid but I will have to disobey you sir,' Mak said.

She avoided Mr. Maranga's eyes.

'Do not be ridiculous young woman. Now you are crossing the line. You know I hate to do this to you very much but it is an order from the Principal. We need to go...I'll drag you if I have to!'

Before Mr. Maranga who had nearly gone through the roof because of the girl's insolence had finished talking, there was a loud explosion from within the mall. Everybody jumped as a bright ball of fire lit the air above the mall. Within no time, people came scrambling from both the front and the back of the mall. Others fell back in incomprehension as they waited for the building to collapse, but nothing more happened. When things calmed down a little, Julie who stood near Mr. Maranga spoke.

'That decides me too sir,' she said facing her teacher. 'I too cannot leave until I know what is the fate of those too girls.'

Outwitted, Mr. Maranga let that ride.

8: The Rescue

The hostages lost count of time as they sat there cold and hungry. They looked like they had been through the wars yet no one apart from the man with a phone had dared take the bread that had been availed to them. The continuous sounds of gunfire that came from outside did not make their waiting any easier. Amy thought it was well past midnight when a loud burst of gunfire came from behind them. The sound was unlike that produced by the guns of the terrorists and for the first time, the little group hurdled there had the first hope of being rescued. It was clear that the sound was coming from different guns. The terrorists seemed to come alive. One of them who was downstairs beyond their view gave a heroic cry before shouting something in guttural Arabic. The one who was guarding them said something in return, then he started shooting from where he was, aiming his gun somewhere downstairs.

'It *is* the army!' the Muslim girl beside Amy said excitedly. 'They've come for us. We'll be rescued...looks like we'll live to tell the tale.'

The terrorist guarding them heard her and shouted for silence over his shoulder. He swung the barrel of his rifle back over the railing and added a fresh magazine then continued shooting.

'The heat is on. They are shooting at the doorway,' the Muslim girl whispered animatedly. 'It appears the army is trying to get in.'

'We need to run. Read between the lines; this is a chance in a million,' Amy said to the other girls quietly.

Raj turned to the women near her.

'Listen,' she told them. 'This is our only chance to get out of here. We must all look for a way out before this shooting stops. If they are cornered, they will turn on us.'

'I have an idea,' Amy said quietly. 'That exit near the toilets, I'll run for it and try to open it, then you'll guide everyone else to follow,' she whispered to Raj.

'Fat chance! They'll shoot you if you try anything like that,' the Muslim girl said.

'I doubt it,' Amy returned. 'I think they are engaged enough not to notice. Besides, we need to run for it immediately!'

She did not wait to hear any of their opinions. She rose and as she crouched, darted quickly towards the toilets. One of the terrorists downstairs saw the movement and shot at her. A hail of bullets followed her all the way to the door of the toilets as bullets rang off the railing and ricocheted off the walls onto the floor all around her. She made it to the toilet just in time as the gunman downstairs turned his gun elsewhere. The one who had been guarding them must have seen her movement but decided he had better fish to fry. She paused for breath in the passageway outside the door of the toilet then darted across to the other door marked 'Emergency Exit'. She quickly unhooked the fire extinguisher and holding it by its top repeatedly hit its grooved base against the padlock. All this time, she was aware that the heavy fire extinguisher's top could come off at any moment and the can would explode taking itself away with her but she tried hard not to think about that; she had to take the chance.

The silver padlock however refused to budge. Amy felt like she had already had her chips. She racked her brains for something to do to no avail. She remembered seeing a blue plastic waste bin in the ladies toilet. She darted inside and quickly emptied the can on the floor, then got out and shut the door firmly behind her. She took the fire extinguished and put it on the floor in the passage leading to the toilet with its top facing the door of the toilet and its grooved base facing the emergency exit on the other side. As quickly as she could and trying hard not to think about what would happen if she failed, she lifted the plastic bin and with all her might brought it down on the top of the fire extinguisher. Nothing happened. She lifted the bin again and brought it down so hard that she went down with it falling on the fire extinguisher itself. There was a loud hiss as the top can of the extinguisher came off. The pressure from the extinguisher propelled it across the passage way

As quickly as she could and trying hard not to think about what would happen if she failed, she lifted the plastic bin and with all her might brought it down on the top of the fire extin-guisher.

taking her with it. It hit the emergency door across the passage and left a gaping hole as it disappeared inside. Amy's head hit against the door and she fell on the floor face first and passed out.

A few moments later, she regained consciousness. Raj was trying to lift her up as the other hostages fought tooth and nail to get through the opening the fire extinguisher had made in the lower part of the emergency exit. The escapees had widened the hole a little.

'Are you alright?' Raj who had already done the spadework asked as she looked down at her friend.

'I think I'll live,' Amy replied groaning and feeling like a small dog in tall weeds. She rubbed her eyes and tried to focus.

'C'mon,' Raj said as she lifted her friend to a sitting position. 'We need to hurry and get out of here. Once the terrorists realize we've escaped, they'll turn on the heat.'

'Where are they?' Amy didn't need to tell her friend who she meant.

'He left us and ran downstairs. I think one of his colleagues has been shot. It won't take him long to realize the way we've gone,' Raj said as she maneuvered her friend through the gaping hole in the lower part of the emergency exit.

All the other hostages with whom they had been held had resorted to a herd mentality; they had already scrambled through, fighting tooth and nail to get out.

'Here,' the Muslim girl said from the semi darkness on the other side of the destroyed door. She maneuvered Amy through the iron bars into the dark room beyond.

Raj squeezed through after her friend. They emerged onto a semi dark room which looked like an air cleaning room. There was shadowed equipment in the low ceilinged room and the machines whirling like an airborne scourge left a cool wind running through the room. When their eyes adapted to the semi darkness, they saw that there were six aluminum air vents that led in several directions. Many of the people who had got there before them had already chosen vents randomly and were crawling through them with all they were made of.

'Which way?' Amy asked.

'I don't know,' the Muslim girl said. 'There's no way of telling where any of them leads.'

'Follow me,' Raj said choosing a vent that led to her left. 'We need to hedge our bets...in case the terrorists come in pursuit.'

Apparently, nobody had gone that way for the wire grill that covered the vent was still in place. She crawled in after pulling off the grill. The vent was just wide enough for her to move her hands and crawl forward snake-like. She crawled ahead in the semi darkness as the other two girls followed. A few metres ahead, the vent curved to the right, then ascended to an upper level. Raj went on cautiously, hooking her fingers and feet to the joints that brought together the aluminum metal pieces that made the air vent. Up ahead, the vent widened as it led to an opening which was covered by a wire grill. There were three air conditioners which were about a square metre each. The fans were still although cool air went through them into the building beyond. Through the wire mesh between them, Raj could see an open area inside the mall. The other two girls crawled over and lay flat beside her.

'Well,' Raj said, 'here we are. This looks like the air feed into this part of the building. I think this area was widened to make it easier to install or repair these air conditioners.'

'That means we're still inside the building,' Amy observed.

'I wonder whether any of those other vents leads outside,' the Muslim girl said.

'I don't think anyone is likely to discover us here,' Raj said. 'I think we should stay put until we are sure the building has been secured.'

Through the wire mesh they could see a corridor with a metal railing like the one downstairs where they had cowered since the afternoon. They couldn't see the floor of the corridor but across the open space, they could see a similar railing on the other side of the open space between. There were several abandoned stands beyond the railing where traders had deserted their businesses as they ran to safety. Amy could see an electronics shop directly across from where they were. It had laptop computers in various sizes and colours, up market mobile phones and other electronic goods she could not make out properly. Next to it was a Jewelers shop that appeared to be a dealer in ladies things. She could see shiny neck chains, watches, and earrings in various colours from bronze, silver to gold. Next to the Jewelers there was a ladies clothes dealer and she could see mannequins displaying all manner of ladies' clothes.

'You didn't tell us who you are,' Raj who was as sharp as a tack told the Muslim girl suddenly.

Amy was caught unawares because it hadn't occurred to her to ask the girl for her name. The circumstances in which they found themselves had relegated human warmth to the background.

'There was hardly any time,' the girl said good-naturedly. 'My name is Aaishah Zainab.'

'Which one of the two do you prefer?' Amy asked her.

'I have no preference. I'm used to being called by the two names together,' she said.

'Can I call you Aisha?' Amy insisted.

'Aaishah,' Zainab corrected her pronunciation by prolonging the 'a' and pronouncing the 'h'. 'Sure, I don't mind.'

'She was the youngest wife of the Prophet. May peace be upon him!' Raj explained.

She felt funny explaining Muslim names while hers was Indian. She had been named on her mother's side although she adored Islam, her father's religion. This way, she felt that the two cultures met, blended and balanced within her.

'Thanks Zainab for what you've done. We understand you didn't have to,' Raj said.

'It is my duty. It would have been the duty of any proper Muslim,' Aaishah explained.

'You can say that again,' Raj agreed.

'What were you doing here if you don't mind my asking?' Raj asked Aaishah.

'I...ah...I'm a student. We had come for a cooking competition which was being held on the roof – at the parking on the roof, if you know where it is,' she replied.

'Shhhh!' Amy suddenly hushed them and the other two girls fell silent and pricked their ears.

In the silence, they heard approaching footsteps. Measured footsteps approached their hideout from the left, then stopped just outside where they were as if somebody was listening. Then there was prolonged silence. Just when Amy was about to dismiss them, they heard them again, now closer to them, then without any warning, a figure suddenly appeared immediately in front of the air conditioner in the middle, right under their noses. They could only see the top part of a green helmet outside as the figure stood listening. Before any of the girls could think of what to do, the figure moved away to stand near the railing as if looking over the railing at a lower floor. Suddenly, it jumped back and away as a burst of gunfire came from downstairs. The bullets ripped into the wall near where the girls were. Some ricocheted and hit the wire mesh and the still air conditioners. The girls scrambled back and lay still. Hurried footsteps rushed to their right as the gunfire was returned. The girls kept completely still as the gunfire continued for several minutes. There was a cry of pain somewhere downstairs followed by silence. It was more than a quarter of an hour later that the three girls had courage enough to stir their muscles which had turned as stiff as hedge-stakes.

Amy looked outside through the wire mesh. In the shops on the other side across from where they lay, she could see a number of uniformed soldiers in jungle camouflage and green helmets like the one they had seen earlier. They were systematically ransacking the shops, putting things into white paper bags and into their pockets. They went into the jewelers shop, then went from shelf to shelf filling their pockets and lining the insides of their jackets. Amy felt aghast at what she was looking at. She thought her eyes were playing tricks on her. Were these the people they were waiting to come and save them?

'Oh my God,' she breathed.

It was clear you could have knocked her down with a feather.

'What is it?' Aaishah asked as she too tried to raise herself and look outside.

'You don't want to know,' Amy said as she held her breath.

'They are looting! The barefaced liars; they tell people they keep security and this is what they do?' Raj voiced her thoughts.

'Yeah, I can't believe they are feathering their nests here this way and putting many hard working citizens out of business!' Amy said.

'Really?' Aaishah wondered. 'Braving terrorist guns to loot as we wait to be saved? Hey, you over here!!' she said as loud as she could.

The soldiers on the other side turned around sharply.

'Shhh!' Raj warned her under her breath. 'We've got to keep a lid on our hideout or word will get out and we'll face the music.'

'True,' Amy whispered silently. 'That could put us in worse danger than that of the terrorists. They don't want any witnesses to what they are doing.'

'Oh God in heaven!' Aaishah said. 'Allah have mercy!'

The three girls kept quiet as they watched the activity on the other side of the building. The soldiers had reacted immediately they heard the shout. They were wary of anyone interrupting their license to print money. They looked around them as if trying to determine where the shout had come from. One of them looked directly at the air conditioners behind which the girls lay and they cringed in fear. If he thought of shooting at them, they were sitting ducks. There was no way of scrambling back or moving anywhere anyway. They held their breath as the soldier looked at the still fans for a long minute. He nudged his colleague who also turned to look. He swung his gun in their direction and held it there for some agonizing moment prepared to shoot if anything moved, then seemed to think better of it. It didn't look like anyone could survive there for long. However, the courage to steal seemed to have ebbed and the soldiers quickly moved onto the other shop, took a number of mobile phones and hurried away. The girls looked aghast as their only chance of getting saved melted away. The soldiers hurried on out of sight leaving the girls feeling caught between Scylla and Charybdis.

'Now what do we do? We can't sit here fine tuning an escape plan, can we?' Aaishah wondered aloud.

'We sit tight and play it by the ear,' Raj whispered. 'This will surely end somehow. What we need to do is keep together.'

'If one of us squeezes and turns around, we can kick one of these air conditioners off and try to crawl through,' Aaishah said.

'I think the problem will be what we crawl out onto,' Raj said. 'We aren't certain what is on the other side.'

'At least there are no terrorists,' Amy said. 'They can't have been on the same floor with those soldiers.'

'That means we should give the soldiers a little while to make good their escape, then we will risk it,' Raj said.

The girls kept quietly listened to the receding footsteps of the soldiers which faded gradually to their right. After a few minutes, the place was as still as a tunnel except for the humming of the air machines down the way they had come. After some time, Raj nodded then crawled over to the tranquil fan to the right and pushed her ear as far as she dared. She listened for some time before she turned to the other girls and whispered to them that the coast was clear; it was time to get their plan off the ground. Aaishah who was in the middle turned slowly as the other two girls squeezed their bodies to the walls of the vent as far as they could to give her room for maneuver. After a long struggle and a lot of sweating, she was able to turn so that her head was facing the way they had come. She then edged near the still fan in the middle and aiming her right leg at its middle area pushed with all her might. It didn't budge. She pushed again, then kicked it moving her knee as far as she could in the little space there was. The girls had to agree it was no use.

'Try to use both legs,' Raj advised her. 'Save your energy by breathing in, then kick it once with both your feet.'

Aaishah moved back a little to give herself space enough for her second leg. She turned on her back and lay there for perhaps a minute. Amy felt apprehensive because it was clear Aaishah had two left feet. Just when Amy was about to ask her whether she had given up, she edged herself near the still fan then pulled both her knees as far back as she could. She took a deep breath then kicked the fan in the middle with all the energy she had left. The fan crashed with a noise as loud as a blast of a mine explosion as both her legs went through. Then the fat hit the fire; the force of her push sent her through the hole and she went crashing through it. The other two girls tried to grab her hands as she went through but they were a second too late. Overshooting her mark, Aaishah fell out through the hole with a loud reverberation of crashing plastic. She landed somewhere beyond the other girls' line of vision. Her crash was followed by a burst of gunfire from somewhere below, then all was still.

'Aaishah?' Raj called silently. There was no response. 'Aaisha,' she called again a bit loudly.

There was a groan outside somewhere. Raj turned and crawled forward slowly, then looked out through the hole. Aaisha had fallen down onto the corridor two and half metres below. Raj saw that the other girl had broken her right leg at the shin as she fell.

'Is she alright?' Amy asked behind her.

'Looks like she has broken her right leg,' Raj returned. 'We've got to go and help her before anyone comes.'

'C'mon then, let's go.'

Raj pushed her head out slowly, looked right and left then crawled out of their hideout. She turned herself at the edge of the gaping hole, then lowered herself on her hands as she held the thick wiring cables which hang out from the hole. She slid herself down until her feet felt the floor. She stood there to regain her breath, then knelt to look at Aishah as she lay groaning silently on the floor. Amy looked down at them from the yawning hole. She turned the way her friend had done then holding onto the cables lowered herself to the floor. She knelt beside Raj as both examined Aaishah.

'Oh my God!' she whispered silently.

'She's going to hell in a handcart...but she'll live. We need to move her quickly,' Raj who was practical to a fault said. 'Any minute someone may come down any of these corridors to investigate the crashing noise and surprise us here.'

'Which way?' Amy whispered.

'That,' Raj pointed her pulled lips down right.

They lifted Aaishah up then taking her between them carried her down the corridor. She groaned feeling like a millstone around the two girls' necks. They turned into the first clothes shop they found, maneuvered her round behind a small glass counter and set her down on the floor. Raj then set about giving Aaishah as good a first aid as she could.

9: Down a Dark Smelly Tunnel

The shop they had gone into was a men's shop that dealt mainly in jeans, corduroys and clothes of such tough material. Raj tried to tie Aaishah using the strips of cloth torn off the garments they found in the shop. They could however not find a bandage soft and long enough to tie the wound.

'Amy, I'm sorry but you'll have to go scouting around for better material,' Raj said. 'You'll also need to get pieces of metal or wood strong enough to hold the leg straight.'

Amy was apprehensive. Going out of the security of their new hide out and leaving her friends was like courting the wrath of the devil. She saw however that to stem Aaishah's bleeding, something had to be done urgently. So agreeing with her friend, she left their hide out and peered outside. For the first time, she saw exactly where they were. They were on the second floor of the building. From where she was, she could see three floors of shops and other businesses. In the middle sheltered area, she saw the elevators they had seen as they went to the corner café with Raj and her mother. It appeared that almost the whole of the first floor was composed of restaurants. She tried to reason out the way they had gone downstairs after their meal. She saw the café they had visited at one corner on the floor below her. That meant that the supermarket where they had spent the afternoon was behind the café. She remembered that they had gone downstairs in order to get into the supermarket and the terrorists had held them hostage on the first floor of the supermarket. That meant that the upper floor of the supermarket must have been behind the counter of the restaurant she could see on the first floor. It meant too that they must have spent the afternoon behind that counter she could see on the first floor. So the vent they had climbed through had led them up one floor to deposit them on the second floor. That was where they were. It made sense. It meant too that if there were no other terrorists apart from the four they had seen, then it was unlikely that any of them had come up here. That was why the soldiers had come up here themselves. It was the reason

Raj tried to tie Aaishah using the strips of cloth torn off the garments they found in the shop.

why they had been calmly looting. Evidence of the death and destruction the terrorists had left in their wake was however clear enough. She could see at least one body on each of the four sides of every floor. The worst scene was at the elevators. Bodies were strewn all over and it appeared that they had piled up and caused it to jam. At its landing on the first floor, it was clear that the terrorists had shot into the crowd that had been trying to get away for bullet riddled bodies were piled on each other. The dark blue hue of the elevator had turned dark grey with congealed blood. The shiny metallic railings on each side of the still elevators were splashed with pink. Amy looked away and gagged as her stomach turned.

She crept cautiously to the other side of the building where she could see a ladies shop and a chemist. Their doors were ajar and goods were strewn all over the place. Interestingly, little appeared to have been taken out of them but the jewelers and the electronic shops had been cleaned out. She went into a chemist and looked around. She took a bottle of antiseptic, then grabbed a roll of cotton wool and some bandages and cautiously began retracing her steps. It was then that she remembered; Raj had asked her to get straight pieces of wood for holding the leg straight. She went in search of them. Since she hadn't come across any where she had been, she decided to try the shops to her left. The entire floor on that side appeared to be a casino of some sort. There were tables with glass tops and many lights that blinked on and off in the semi darkness. Finding nothing useful by the time she had gone to the end of the long room that housed the casino, she had no option but to go downstairs to the lower floor to try there. As she emerged onto the first floor landing, gunfire erupted somewhere to her left beyond a door marked 'exit'. She guessed it led to the stairs then to the ground floor. She stood there confused a split second before the door burst open and one of the terrorists came rushing in – it was clear he had gone ballistic. Her heart sank. She screamed as the terrorist ran towards her, grabbed her by the neck and dragged her towards another exit far to their right. More gunfire followed behind the cafe on the first floor and she realized that there was a heavy fight inside the supermarket. She could not scream any more for the terrorist had clamped his hand tightly across her mouth gagging out any sound. As they got to the end of the corridor leading to the other exit, Raj called her desperately from the floor above.

'Amy? Amy?'

She whimpered as she tried to shout. The terrorist looked up in the direction the voice had come from and going off the deep end, he shot a round of bullets at her. They rang off the wall and the metal railing along the corridor of the second floor. As he leaned forward to shoot again, Amy slipped from under his arm and tried to run. He tripped her as he swung the rifle and brought it down on her head. The butt of the gun caught her on the back of her head and she crashed head long to the floor and passed out.

From the second floor, Raj looked down cautiously as the burst of gunfire stopped. She saw the terrorist looking up but he could not see her. Her friend lay on the floor curled up in a heap. She racked her brains as she sought what to do to save her friend. She considered her options. She could not attack the terrorist single handedly yet she could not stay indefinitely on the second floor. The terrorist knew she was there and he would definitely come up to get her. There didn't appear to be anyone else on the second floor apart from her and the injured Aaishah. Aaishah herself continued to groan in pain where she had left her drawing attention to them. She looked down again. The terrorist didn't seem any longer bothered about her. Instead, he had taken out a string of grenades from his backpack and was walking along the corridor on the first floor stooping to do something she couldn't see clearly every five metres or so. What was he doing? She looked again but she couldn't determine what was going on. Meanwhile, gunfire raged on downstairs especially on the ground floor. It appeared that some rescuers had come in through the main entrance near Artcafe, the terrace café outside the mall entrance, and were trying to pin the terrorists to the first floor. The thick of the battle appeared to be inside the supermarket and around the elevators under her. She looked down onto the first floor again. The terrorist was still busy with his bag. She watched as he raised the front metal shutter of a shop, removed something from his bag, bit at it - bit at it? - and then wedged it under the door.

It occurred to her that the terrorist was setting up grenades around the first floor. Aaishah's words came back to her. She had said that according to what the terrorists had said in Arabic, they had been wiring up the building. And then the harsh terrorist had told them to sit tight for they were all going down together. Going down together? It was now clear. They were intent on causing as much damage as possible. They wanted to kill as many people as possible too! And the soldiers who had come in didn't know! But how could they? They had seemed more intent on lining their pockets than securing the building. While they thought they were pinning the terrorists to the upper floors, the terrorists were really drawing them on into the heart of the building so that they could bring the building down. She remembered reading about how the American embassy had been blown up from within – from the underground parking lot; and how the twin towers had been brought down in New York. It was a pattern. And here they wanted to draw as many people as possible into the building and then bring down the building to kill themselves with as many people as they could. And they wanted soldiers – possibly to reduce the number of them fighting in Somalia.

It occurred to her that they had to be stopped come hell or high water. If the terrorist blew up the building and got out, it would be plain sailing for him after that. But how could they be stopped by a simple defenseless school girl, barehanded? It was crazy. She looked down at her friend who still lay prostrate on the corridor of the first floor. Was she dead? Had she mothered her for eight months only to bring her to this? She would be stillborn? It was unbelievable. And as she sat here impotent, the terrorist continued to string a necklace of grenades around the first floor. She looked again. He was no longer on the first floor. He had climbed to the second and he continued his gruesome task in which he was so absorbed that it did not occur to him to first find out what had happened to her. Or maybe he didn't care? Yes, that was it. He knew she was a toothless dog who could not stand up to him. She was just waiting on the second floor so that he could come and put a bullet through her head. Raj felt tears at the corner of her eyes. So much wasted; time, money, love and what else? Maybe the question was what not else. She had to do something. She could not die in vain; her friend had not died in vain. She felt tears rolling down her cheeks but she did not try to stop them. She did not know exactly how long she sat there or at what point she made her resolve. She only found herself crawling like a snake across the floor. She instinctively knew that when the terrorist came near where Aaishah was, he would hear her whimpering. She knew that he would be curious to find out what it was, or he would simply be drawn to her by the need to kill her. If the terrorist decided to look into the shop where she was, Raj decided it would be safe to play possum. She had less than five minutes to act.

She crawled back into the room where she had left Aaishah. She was still in pain and appeared to be growing delirious. She took a long strip of makeshift bandage and tied it across her mouth securing it properly behind her head. Aaishah would have to hold on until this little task was done. 'I can't help it,' Raj thought to herself. 'There is no other way.' She then dragged her out of the shop to the door. She looked across at the terrorist who was absorbed in his ghastly task on the other side. On one corner of the corridor near where they were, there was a recessed pillar which supported the railing. If she leaned Aaishah there, she would be out of site. If the terrorist heard her whimpers and decided to come and investigate, he would be compelled to come all the way round before he discovered where Aaishah was.

And to do that, if the terrorist kept the route he was keeping around the second floor, he would be compelled to come and stand outside the door of the shop she and Aaishah had been. It was all a gamble but it was the best she could do. She had to leave the rest to God.

Gunfire still raged downstairs but the terrorist on the other side of the second floor seemed less concerned about it. It occurred to Raj that the other terrorists might have been keeping the rescuers busy down there until their colleague was finished with his dirty work; then they would withdraw and throw a single grenade and the whole building would come tumbling down. Again, she felt that she could not let it happen. She watched as the terrorist rounded the corner to her left, then came down the corridor towards her. He stopped outside a barber shop, looked through a window then wedged a grenade against it and moved on. Somewhere downstairs someone called out 'Omar!' then said something in a language she didn't understand. The terrorist shouted something in return then continued down the corridor. Raj watched him come as she hid behind the counter of the shop in which she was. She held tightly onto the leg of a mannequin which she had plucked off one of the mannequins in the shop. She knew she had to do it; it was mind over matter.

The terrorist came down the corridor shuffling his feet. He held a grenade in his hand and as he approached, he pulled out the pin using his teeth. He appeared bent on doing something quickly and then joining his friends downstairs. A few metres away, he heard Aaishah's moans and slackened his pace as he raised his gun so that his right eye was looking down the barrel. He approached cautiously then stopped and peered slowly around the pillar against which Aaishah was leaning. He looked at the black gown she wore and the flowered scarf wound around her head and relaxed. He said something to her but Aaishah moaned in reply. Raj edged out of the shop quietly and holding the leg of the mannequin in both hands, she swung it hard in an anti-clockwise direction and caught the terrorist on his right jaw. He did not even have time to get surprised. He went over the railing losing his grip on the grenade he held so that it went over the railing first and he followed it. He fell down the three floors to the ground. Before Raj could look down to see where he had fallen, the grenade exploded throwing debris as high as where she was as the building trembled. The shock threw her against the wall and she hit her head against the ledge and fell to the floor of the corridor.

When the air cleared a little, she rose and peered down at the floors below. The first thing she saw through the rising smoke was the gaping hole ripped in the middle of the open area on the ground floor. The body of the terrorist had been blown into smithereens. On the first floor, the terrorist who had called the other was rising from the floor cursing loudly. He looked around trying to get his bearings, then walked unsteadily towards the end of the corridor. Raj looked where Amy had fallen and saw that she was trying to rise too. She was alive!

'Amy! Amy!' she called.

Amy didn't seem to hear her nor did she appear aware of the immediate danger facing her. As Raj looked, the terrorist pulled out a pistol and walked over where Amy was trying to get her bearing. He grabbed Amy by her hair then holding the pistol against her temple dragged her beyond Raj's line of vision as he swore in a foreign tongue.

'Amy! Amy!' Raj called again as she struggled towards the spiral staircase at the end of the corridor holding her dizzy head in her hands. She took the steps quickly as she held on to the railing with one hand to steady herself. On the first floor landing, she saw the exit at the other end where a swinging door told her that was the way the terrorist had gone. Amy was nowhere in sight. She approached the door carefully. The door opened on to a flight of stairs. A trail of blood told her that the terrorist had dragged Amy downstairs. She could hear some noise coming from down the stairs as if something was being dragged down the stairs. She went down carefully pausing now and then to listen. On the ground floor landing, she peered round at the open area leading to the elevators and the corridors fronting the various businesses. The explosion had ripped water pipes out of the ground and the area around the ground floor was quickly flooding with water. There was no one in sight. As she wondered where the terrorist might have gone, she heard some noise coming from the basement. It sounded like a woman in pain calling for help. She paused and listened; it was Amy's voice and she was calling out to her. She hadn't realized there was a basement. She went down the wet stairs carefully pausing again and again to listen. The terrorist didn't know she was following him. She realized that her strength lay in not alerting him she was on his trail otherwise her rescue plan would go belly up.

The stairs opened onto a car park. The little water coming from up the stairs was flowing in a trickle to her left. Vehicles were parked bumper to bumper and there was little space for maneuver between the bumpers and the wall. It must have been a busy day, she mused. She knew there was another car park on top of the building which customers preferred to this. In fact, she had always assumed that the top one was the only parking lot. She remembered Aaishah saying there had been a competition of some sort there. Maybe that was why vehicles had been diverted here. She looked across the parking but she couldn't see any movement. She knelt down carefully and cautiously looked under the cars. There was nobody in sight. She was about to rise when she noticed something. There were wet footprints leading to the right; and there were drops of blood too. I must reach that girl in a hurry, she thought. She kept feeling that she had given Amy the short end of the stick by sending her for bandages.

She walked carefully to her right, stooping a little to examine the direction of the footprints. It felt like an uphill battle all the way. The footprints led directly right between the wall of the basement parking and the bumpers of a number of off-road vehicles whose dusty bumpers and rims told her they hadn't moved for some time. The wet footsteps went straight ahead for several metres then the trail ran cold. She stood there wondering where the terrorist might have gone. He could not have gone out of the parking lot through the door because the black and yellow stripped barriers were still in place and there was no guard in sight. In any case, she thought, the time taken to drag a wounded girl across the parking would have been too long and she would have found them here. No, there must be some other way. But where? She already felt she was fighting a losing battle. There were no doors. The only exit apart from the barriers was the stairs down which she had come. She looked around perplexed. Could two human beings really melt into thin air like that? Maybe she wasn't given to find them; she didn't have the expertise. Amy, I'm sorry I have failed you, she thought her knees beginning to buckle, her eyes clouding with tears. She sat down and leaned her back against the wall of the basement. Amy! Her child of eight months stillborn! Aborted! She held her head in her hands and began waiting for whatever was in store for her. She would go down in history as the most irresponsible mother who had ever lived, she thought to herself as she slumped against the wall to lick her wounds because she had no plan B.

It might have been the way she was sitting that gave her the idea. Or it could have been sheer luck; this she'd never be able to tell. Or it could simply have been Allah come to her aid at her greatest hour of need! From the corner of her left eye, she noticed a red pulley on which was wound the red rubber hoses used to put out fire. She thought the pulley was sitting at a weird angle. It was tilted slightly rather than be parallel to the wall as it should have been. It looked like it had somehow come off and the repair work had been amateurish so that the only centre bolt which fixes such pulleys to the wall was loose. Loose? She wasn't sure. She rose and cautiously walked towards the pulley. When she was near enough, she realized that the pulley was fixed onto a wooden platform. The curious angle of the pulley resulted from the fact that the wooden platform itself had come of the wall. No, it was some kind of trapdoor on which the pulley was fixed. And it looked like the trapdoor had recently been fixed there. She reached out and pulled at it carefully. It swung outwards without a sound. She peered inside.

What hit her first was the dirty dank smell of a disused sewer. There was a long dark tunnel at the end of which was a very faint light. She listened carefully. Somebody was moaning in there; it was a young woman's voice. Better late than never, she thought. She crept into the tunnel carefully, then stopped to listen. She then swung the trapdoor carefully to which left her in darkness. She crawled forward on all fours as the moaning sounds came nearer and nearer. It *was* Amy. It was her daughter. She could not risk calling until she was sure Amy was alone. She crawled forward inch by inch as her eyes slowly adjusted to the darkness. Ahead, she could make out a figure lying on its back. It was the mourning form and there appeared to be no one else within the vicinity. She crawled forward and touched the foot.

'Amy? Amy? Is that you?' she whispered.

'Raj, that's you?' Amy moaned wearing her heart on her sleeve.

'Allah is great. He has saved you! Are you badly hurt?'

'Thank god it is you, Raj. I'll live, don't worry, but don't let him!'

'Him? Where is he?'

'He's gone on further ahead - towards the sound of water at the end of the tunnel. He is wounded and I think his gun is out.'

'Hold still, I'm coming back.'

'Be careful,' Amy said as Raj crawled ahead.

She thanked her lucky stars that the terrorist had abandoned her there without killing her.

10: A Reunion

As she came near the end of the tunnel, Raj heard the sound of flowing water quite distinctly. She could not see or hear anyone. At the very edge of the tunnel, she peered out. Ahead of her was a three-metre wide tunnel flowing with dirty murky water. Above it directly in front of her was what looked like a bridge although she couldn't hear any traffic on it. There was no one in sight. She looked back into the tunnel.

'Amy?' she called, 'Are you sure anyone came down this way?'

'Check everywhere properly. I'm sure he went out that way,' Amy said in the darkness behind her.

'It's some sort of dirty stream here and there is no one. It is not deep enough to swim under,' Raj returned.

'Go on quickly. You are wasting time. There is no other way and you must inform people who can apprehend him,' she sounded weak and Raj realized she had to hurry and get help for her.

Amy on the other hand did not tell her friend how she admired her. Her individual courage, bravery and resolve was the shape of things to come; it was what would be required to fight terrorism.

Raj crawled out of the tunnel carefully and stepped into the dirty water. It was not exactly a sewer. It appeared that the tunnel had been dug out here to take care of flood waters from upper Nairobi. It occurred to her too that the building of the parking lot she had left behind had probably been done during a dry year. Later, probably during a year when the heavens really opened, the management had realized the necessity of building a tunnel which could be used to clear food waters out of the parking lot – in case flood waters came that far. It might even have flooded once or twice before they came up with the idea of the tunnel. How the terrorists had discovered the tunnel and realized they could wreak havoc and escape this way was a mystery. The attack of the mall must have been partly an inside job. Raj remembered the Muslim man with the phone on the first floor where they had been held. That looked like an inside job itself.

As she came near the end of the tunnel, Raj heard the sound of flowing water quite distinctly. She could not see or hear anyone.

She cast her eyes down the tunnel as far as the eye could see. It curved to the left about fifty metres ahead. An injured man could not have gone down that far in the little time between coming out of the building less than ten minutes ago and now. She cast her eyes in the opposite direction. The tunnel went straight ahead. On the left side of the tunnel were tall three metre iron sheets fencing off some kind of construction site. None of the iron sheets looked out of place. On the opposite bank, there was a good metre or two of properly manicured stretch of grass which extended to a tall impenetrable *K-apple* hedge. The fence itself was well trimmed and extended as far as the eye could see. The terrorist was even more unlikely to have gone that way. She turned right and sloshed through the murky water until she was well clear of the bridge. She crawled up the grassy bank and looked onto a small deserted bridge. There was a paved road that led in both directions. She saw the imposing block that was the Westgate Mall on the other side of the road. Where the hell had he gone? There was no escape route this way. She walked unsteadily on to the road and looked in both directions. To her right, the road wound up to some living quarters ahead. It looked like a cul-de-sac - which was deserted. She turned to her left.

The road led up for about a hundred metres. There was some yellow tape about fifty metres ahead which marked a police cordon. Beyond the police cordon she could see a barrage of press people lounging about. There were cameras on tripods. This meant, she thought, that there was news coming from this direction, from behind the mall. It was quite likely that this was the way that many of the survivors came. It was ironical that no one was looking in her direction. No one had seen her yet. But the man he sought was nowhere in sight. She was about to turn and go scouting elsewhere when, from the left side of the road about twenty metres away, emerged a bloodied figure. He started shouting as he hobbled slowly towards the press and the police beyond. His shouting attracted the people at the end of the street.

'Help! Help!' he cried trying to feed them a line. 'I'm wounded, I'm shot!'

The noise he raised drew attention to Raj too as she followed after him. She looked carefully at him. It was the terrorist she had seen on the first floor, the very man who had yanked Amy by her hair and dragged her out through the stairs. He had changed out of the bloodied blue shirt and dark trousers. He now wore a light blue track suit and a sports cap. His clothes were bloody and there was a rip on the left leg of his trousers. He had also shed his head scarf and the bag he had carried behind his back. The bullet belt was also nowhere in sight. But there was no mistaking both the thin weasel face and the gait. He was hoping to use the confusion to get himself off the hook.

'Arrest him!' she shouted as she saw a couple of policemen jump over the cordon and head for the hobbling, screaming figure.

Her shouts attracted his attention too for he was barely fifteen metres away. He got a rude awakening and spun around like one who had been hit on the back. He looked at her like she was a bat out of hell.

'You!' he shouted. 'Shut up or I'll blow your brains out!'

He drew a gun out of his pocket. The policemen held back as they too drew out their weapons.

'Drop your gun or we will drop you!' someone shouted.

The terrorist turned to face Raj. He seemed undecided for a split second, then he put the barrel of the pistol into his mouth and pulled the trigger. There was a loud report then the man collapsed onto the street. The police seemed to see her then.

'Hands in the air!' someone said.

Raj raised her hands as she felt her knees grow weak and slowly she sank to the ground. She must have been out for a few minutes for when she opened her eyes, the face of Mr. Maranga was looking down at her.

'Miss Manji, are you okay?' he asked as he squinted at her.

She saw several other faces crowd about her. She was lying on a stretcher and paramedics were thumbing her on the face and arms. She sat up and saw the familiar faces of her schoolmates whose eyes feasted on her and the light blue St Mary's uniform. A number applauded. They were over the moon.

'Wait till we give her first aid,' someone said and she was pushed to a lying position again.

'I'm alright,' Raj said trying to sit up again. 'Please, Amy. She's in the tunnel down there. She is injured. I think she has been shot.'

'Don't worry. There are people there. They'll take care of her,' one paramedic tried to assure her.

'You don't understand,' she insisted as she tried to rise. 'There's a hidden tunnel under that bridge. It is not easy to find her.'

This time someone listened and called a police officer. Raj got off the stretcher as the paramedics tried to restrain her. She hobbled over to meet the policeman and briefed him about where to find Amy and Aaishah. She insisted she had to accompany the police for there was little time. She led a squad of officers down the road towards the bridge. They helped her to the entrance to the underground parking lot where she pointed out the way to the stairs and the hidden tunnel through which the terrorist had tried to escape. Within five minutes, Amy was extracted from the tunnel and led away from the building to receive medical attention. She had not been shot but she had suffered concussion and had injuries to the arms and legs. The doctors said she was out of danger. Aaishah was also fetched out of the second floor where Raj had left her. She had passed out but the doctor said that the first aid Raj had given her would ensure she would recover. Without it, the doctor said, she would have bled to death. Raj escorted Amy to the ambulance. The two girls gripped their hands tightly. It was only when the ambulance left, after the doctors had assured her that Amy was out of danger that she allowed the doctors to attend to her. As she shut her eyes, she listened to the words of Paul Simon singing somewhere;

> *No I would not give you false hope*
> *On this strange and mournful day*
> *But the mother and child re-union*

Is only a motion away...
The rescue was already done and dusted.

Epilogue

'Hey, have you forgotten?' the white girl told the girl next to her. They sat at the back of the class on the left side of the class.

'Forgotten what?' the other girl said without looking up from the book she was reading. She was a stout girl with a hint of red pimples on her cheeks and her forehead.

'Over lunch you said you had a bone to pick...with Stella remember?'

'Oh, that,' she said brightening up. 'You are sure we have the time for that Julie? BB is just about here.'

'Sure. The mood of this class needs uplifting I think,' Julie said. 'Besides, there is definitely a minute or two.'

'Fine,' the other girl said.

The stout light-skinned girl stood up and walked down to the front of the class. She wore glasses with a hue of tint which made it difficult to see the expression in her eyes. She swayed from side to side as she walked holding her hands at her hips and swinging her hips from side to side. She walked over to the row on the right where she stood before a dark girl. The other girl looked up at the newcomer in incomprehension.

'Hi Stella,' she said as she adjusted her glasses so that she looked at the other girl above the rims. Her eyes were a little red and the left eye appeared to have a hint of a squint.

'Hi Raj,' the other girl said still looking up in incredulity.

'Oh sorry to come to you this unannounced but the last time I checked, I had promised to come pick up my book remember?'

The other girl simply smiled at her. The girl called Raj picked a voluminous copy of *Prentice Hall Literature* that the girl called Stella had been reading. She considered it for some time, then raised it up in the air as she looked up there at it comically. She looked at the class. Her little act did not produce the desired results from the rest of the

class and she wondered why. She darted her eyes to the door to make
sure it was not Mr. Maranga come in at the wrong time all over again.

The girl called Raj picked a voluminous copy of Prentice Hall Literature that the girl called Stella had been reading. She considered it for some time, then raised it up in the air···

'What!' she said as she looked round the class.

She made sure that the class understood she expected no answer. The other students simply stared stonily back at her as she lowered the voluminous book back onto Stella's desk.

'Hey, say something!' she told the rest of the class.

No one spoke though they were all looking back at her. Something fell heavily to the floor near her feet and she cast her eyes quickly back to Stella. She saw that it was the volume of *Prentice Hall Literature* which she had put back on Stella's desk which had fallen to the floor. She bent to pick it up. As she did, the other girls rose quickly so that by the time she had straightened up, everyone was on her feet.

'Surprise!!' the whole class shouted.

Raj's skin broke into goose pimples as she spun around. The door had opened and Mrs. Mantu, their Maths teacher stood in the doorway looking at her with a knowing look in her eyes.

'Yes, quite a surprise Miss. Manji,' the teacher said as the girl quickly tried to find her tongue.

'I..I..I'm sorry Madam. It is not what it looks like,' she stammered.

It was then that she noted the other faces crowding slowly at the doorway. She saw her friend Amy from 1W first, then there was Ruth and Audrey, her dorm captains and Jenny, her cube mate from 4Y and...what the hell was this about? She noted too that other students from other classes were looking into 2W through the windows. What kind of humiliation was this, she wondered. The crowd at the door parted slowly in a kind of slow motion leaving a space in the doorway on both sides of the standing Maths teacher, then Mrs. Mantu stood aside herself. Raj began trembling as she felt her feet begin to buckle. It was then that she saw Ms. Konga enter, her hands held behind her back. Fine, she thought. At least it was beginning to make sense. She had imitated teachers for long enough and it was no secret in 2W but she wondered just why none of her friends had warned her in time. What the hell had she thought she was doing?

The Principal took about three steps into the classroom as Raj waited for her to utter some word of condemnation – and why the hell was Ms. Konga smiling? Rather than come straight into the class like she had expected, Ms. Konga stood aside and beckoned on to somebody else. Raj looked. It was Amina! The lady who had accompanied her to the hospital that cold September morning, the deputy OCS at Parklands police station! What the hell did she want here? Amina walked into the classroom in very deliberate steps. Raj wondered what this might be about. But Amina, like Ms. Konga did not come all the way into the classroom. She took four deliberate steps, then stood aside beside Ms. Konga and she too beckoned to someone else. Raj waited, her heart in her mouth, her face drenched in cold sweat. Indeed what could all this be about? A very light-skinned lady who looked Swahili or Somali and who was in a black Muslim bui bui entered. What now! Was this about religion? Her being a Muslim? The lady seemed familiar somehow but she could not place her. Then the windows began lightening! What was happening? Was she dreaming or was someone playing a stupid prank on her?

The tall light-skinned lady walked deliberately and came to stand in front of her. She towered above her making her feel all the more a midget than she already was, her nervous nature notwithstanding.

'Hi, Miss Manji, how are you doing?' the lady smiled boldly down at her.

She felt very small. The whole performance was a little over the top. One need not say she had absolutely no words, so she simply looked up at her and tried to find her tongue. She tried desperately to place the face which she felt sure she had seen or met somewhere before.

'My name is Amina Mohammed.' The name did not ring a bell. 'If you still don't recognize my face, I'm the Cabinet Secretary for International Affairs.'

Cabinet Secretary? What the hell was cabinet secretary?

'I'm here to pass on to you the congratulations of the President of the Republic of Kenya for playing your part in saving our country from terrorism.'

Things began to click into place. The face was from the papers. She had seen it often, many of which times it was behind press cameras. The people gathered around her did not let her think through. Cameras were clicking and blinding her as her school mates echoed the school song in unison. Though the whole of 2W was having a field day, Julie could not hold back any longer. She came forward and tried to lift her in the air. Seeing her inability to do so, Mak jumped forward and held Raj on the other side and they both lifted her high up in the air. It began to dawn on Raj by degrees that she had bagged another feather for her cap.

'I'm sorry to interrupt but we can't finish it here,' Ms. Konga said bedding over backwards, 'Let's go to the Shah Hall!'

Before that had properly sunk in, Amy shouted, 'Madam, can I be allowed to carry her to the hall? She is *my* mother!'

Ms. Konga didn't appear to get that quickly enough but Amy got her wish. She took her mother on her back amid her protests and went out of the door as the rest of their school mates followed cheering and singing the school song. Raj was amazed. She felt like a million dollars. Just outside 2W, the first sight she saw was the red carpet extending to the left along the corridor. The next sight was her beaming parents who were waiting there for her! All the teachers were waiting outside for her and so was the rest of the school. She realized that Julie had played her the whole morning. She had found reasons to keep her away from the side of the school they now faced and it appeared she had the tacit nod of the rest of the school including the administration. The decorations and all the other preparations could not have been done in an hour.

Raj had changed the face of St. Mary's. Amy carried her friend on her back as they went down the corridor, past the notice boards and the staffroom where the teachers lining both sides of the corridor cheered her, past 1W and round the corner past the other two Form One classes. They crossed the space between the Form One block and the Shah Hall where Raj was surprised to find a group of Indian women in traditional garb. They broke into song and dance as she emerged from the Form One block. Her daughter took her into the hall where she put her down onto the red carpet at the door. The hall which had been licked into shape was already packed though it could sit a thousand, and a few more at a pinch. Ms. Konga was already there to stay the young girl until the guest of honour went through one of the side doors, walked to the podium and was ready to receive her. Then, as the hall applauded and the students who could not get sitting space in the hall squeezed at the side doors to witness history, Ms. Konga slowly walked the young girl down the aisle to the podium. No bride had been as overwhelmed as she was as she made the twenty metre walk to the front of the hall where the Cabinet Secretary waited. Then she leaned forward.

'I, Amina Zahra Mohamed, the Cabinet Secretary for Foreign Affairs of the Republic of Kenya, on behalf of the President of the Republic of Kenya, have the pleasure to present to you, Dhrupti Manji Rajah, with the Presidential Medal of Honour, for your role in preventing terrorism in this country. This medal comes coupled with a scholarship for you to study at any university of your choice around the world and up to any level of education that you may personally choose. Let this be an inspiration to other patriotic citizens like you and a symbol that should tell all citizens that this country belongs to us all regardless of our religious, historical, geographical or other affiliations.' The applause that followed went on as if it would continue till kingdom come. Raj had undeniably put another one under her belt. Every dog has its day, she thought as she faced the school with her eyes brimming with tears of joy. She was already feeling the world was her oyster.

Also by Jorges P. Lopez
St. Maryan Seven Series

Amy the St. Maryan
St. Maryan Seven and the Soccer Affair
St. Maryan Seven and the Shanghaier
St. Maryan Seven and the Dubai Allure
St. Maryan Seven and the Flying Saucer

Jimmy Karda Series

Jimmy
Jimmy and his Ancestor
Jimmy and Goliath
Jimmy and the Ramshackle
Jimmy and the Dodger
Jimmy and the Hawaiian Shirt
Jimmy and Chiggah
Jimmy and the Cross Customer

Don't miss out!

Visit the website below and you can sign up to receive emails whenever Jorges P. Lopez publishes a new book. There's no charge and no obligation.

https://books2read.com/r/B-A-TWNBB-CGVQC

BOOKS 2 READ

Connecting independent readers to independent writers.

Did you love *St. Maryan Seven The Westgate Rescue*? Then you should read *Amy*[1] by Jorges P. Lopez!

[2]

We have all got to that point where we are about to engage in something new...and we are not sure how to continue. We have all had that chance when we go to a new school or a new class and we are afraid of the reception. Some of our parents have dotted on us in basic or primary school...until it gets to a point when we have to leave them and manage on our own...

AMY is a COMING OF AGE novella in which a teenage girl gets to that point where she has to do an exam in order to join high school, only that our Amy has to go to a boarding school far away from home. She has been used to having things done for her...almost, and now she has to learn to cope on her own. And she has to make new friends.

---

1. https://books2read.com/u/3nGp65

2. https://books2read.com/u/3nGp65

Her passing her exam becomes a stepping stone to a new challenge. But she eventually finds high school a lot more fun than she had ever anticipated.

AMY is the FIRST novella in the ST MARYAN SEVEN SERIES. They tell stories that challenge teenagers about their perceptions, their choices, and give teachers and parents dealing with teenagers tips on how to manage them. AMY introduces the characters who feature in the series as well as grounds the narratives. Besides, this series teaches English Idioms as used in context, thereby helping the teenager improve in communication skills and creative writing. The idea here is that a second language is learnt more easily and quicker through narratives, not the textbook. Welcome aboard.

About the Author

Jorges P. Lopez has been teaching Literature in high schools in Kenya and Communication at The Cooperative University in Nairobi. He has been writing Literary Criticism for more than fifteen years and fiction for just over ten years. He has contributed significantly to the perspective of teaching English as a Second Language in high school and to Communication Skills at the college level. He has developed humorous novellas in the *Jimmy Karda Diaries Series* for ages 9 to 13 which make it easier for learners of English to learn the language and the *St. Maryan Seven Series* for ages 13 to 16 which challenge them to improve spoken and written language. His interests in writing also spill into Poetry, Drama and Literary Fiction. He has written literary criticism books on Henrik Ibsen, Margaret Ogola, Bertolt Brecht, John Steinbeck, John Lara, Adipo Sidang' and many others.